Leave of Absence

Leave of Absence

S. Renée Bess

To my father, who read *Aesops Fables* to me during the *good* times, and who invented stories for me at the *best* times.

To my mother, who bought me my first story book about monkeys and hats, and invited me to sit down and read in the livingroom.

To my sister, who reads every chance that she gets, because she learned early on that the world of books is so wonderful.

To my life's love, Vivian, who shows me every day that anything is possible, and that we have no limitations.

ONE

Kinshasa Jordan looked around the living room of the two bedroom apartment that would be her home for the next year and a half. She walked over to the fireplace, wondering how long it had been since the chimney was last cleaned, and made a mental note to ask the landlord. She liked looking at the bookcases that flanked the hearth. Pressing down on the shelves to test their reliability, she knew which chore she would tackle next.

Although Kinshasa had put quite a few of her things in storage, she had brought a few of her favorite keepsakes with her: a shell from a beach in Maui, two female busts from Kenya, a mixed wood what-not box from Brazil, and some photos of her family. These things, she figured, would give her a sense of home, a center in her new surroundings. They would add texture and warmth to the almost military uniformity of her texts and other books.

Next, Kinshasa inspected the kitchen and dining room. Both were small, but adequate. Kinshasa didn't enjoy cooking, and considered that activity a waste of time. Why cook when she could be writing? She nodded approvingly at the microwave oven perched atop one of the counters, and planned to fill the freezer with microwave dinners for those days when she had to remain on campus late, or the nights when the word processor claimed all of her attention and time.

She walked back through the living room to inspect the furniture that had arrived that afternoon. The moving men placed the Haitian cloth sleep sofa, the two side chairs and the cocktail table exactly where she had directed. Although it would be quite a while before she hung up the few pieces of art she'd brought with her, she was already contemplating where they should go. She stood at one end of the room, surveying the scene, and smiled at its order and balance. One thing that she needed in her life now was order and the balanced feeling that order gave her. She craved an end to the disarray that had surrounded her before her arrival in Allerton.

Boxes stacked up neatly along the hall wall called to her. Her literature notes and teaching materials were in the boxes closest to the smaller bedroom, the one she would use as her office. The other boxes contained linens, clothing, books, tapes and an unfinished manuscript or two.

Three hours later into this March afternoon, Kinshasa sat down on her bed and pondered what she had gotten herself into . . . a contract to teach creative writing at Allerton University during the pre-summer session, and a literature course during the fall and spring semesters.

The offer to teach at Allerton had arrived just as she was caught between the flush of fame following the release of her third novel, and the pain of separating from someone she had once loved so fiercely. The two events, timed as they were, plunged her into a vortex of emotions. Kinshasa grabbed the opportunity to teach at Allerton as if it were a lifeboat. She'd decided abruptly to take a leave of absence from the New Haven Connecticut high school where she had taught for what seemed like forever. She craved a slower pace, older students, different surroundings. And Allerton University provided all of that, plus a respectable escape from chaos . . . from Michael.

Anxious to fill the bookshelves, but aware of her hunger pangs, Kinshasa decided to go out in search of a meal. She walked down the short hallway and went into the bathroom. The mirror above the wash basin reflected her copper brown face. Expressive dark eyes stared back at her. Her nose, often pinched during her childhood by her grandmother, ("Child, whenever you're just sitting around not doing anything, pinch your nose. It'll grow straighter!") rebelled against any artificial stimuli to be aquiline. It was, plain and simple, an African-American nose.

Her mouth held an expression of guarded optimism more readily than a smile. Any smile from Kinshasa was a gift. It had to start in her mind. From there, the smile traveled to her heart. If she were really amused, and the smile could survive the trip, it would voyage from her heart and take up residence on her lips, for all the world to see.

Kinshasa smoothed her hair with three passes of the comb and two flat handed pats. Three weeks after a haircut, arranging her unstraightened hair was more a matter of maintaining the shape than arranging its style. She hoped that she could find an Afro-friendly hair salon in the little burg of Allerton. If not, Philadelphia wasn't that far away.

She picked up her shoulder bag and made a last appraisal of the apartment. She wondered what Michael would think of her new place. Inevitably, something would be wrong. There was no way that Kinshasa could ever please Michael completely.

The mid-afternoon sun promised enough hours of sunlight for her to trust walking toward the town center instead of driving. Kinshasa's sixth sense of personal safety assured her that that part of Allerton was secure.

She passed by boutiques, a pharmacy, some antique and consignment shops, an ice cream emporium overflowing with customers despite the cool edge the breeze held, a printing service business, several cafes, a bar or two and a music store broadcasting an old Phyllis Hyman song. Kinshasa's appetite slowed down, allowing her to enjoy the music, but to feel that same gnawing regret that she always felt when she heard Phyllis Hyman's now stilled voice. That sense of loss for all the songs that Phyllis never had a chance to imbue with her own vocal stamp. She noticed the mix of people on the street, and was pleased to see herself reflected in a few of the faces.

After another two blocks, Kinshasa turned right for no particular reason. An awning protruding from a building midway down the street commanded her attention. The LUNA NEGRA restaurant beckoned. It stood out against its neighbor, a small cafe with a discreetly written,"MKDN'S PLACE", printed neatly on its front door.

Once inside the restaurant, Kinshasa was seated by an efficient and friendly young woman. The LUNA NEGRA seemed to be a restaurant where one could linger and feel welcomed. After ordering her meal from a smiling but not inappropriately warm waitress, Kinshasa looked around and confirmed what she had heard about the Allerton community; that it was an unusual oasis of diversity and tolerance. She felt comforted seeing tables of African-Americans and other people of color who could have been Hispanic or Middle Eastern interspersed with whites.

As she began eating, she noticed that she wasn't the only person dining alone. There were a few tables of solo diners. One, a handsome lone black woman, offered her a smile. Kinshasa estimated that the woman was about her own age. She admired her stylishly cut tight curls. Kinshasa thought that she saw a momentary flicker of curiosity dance about the woman's eyes. She nodded her acknowledgment of the stranger's smile, and then looked down at her nearly empty plate.

"All finished here?" The waitress removed the dish.

"Yes, thanks. Everything was delicious."

"I'll tell the chef. Would you like some coffee or dessert?"

Kinshasa considered the offer. "No. Just the check, please."

Anxious to return to her apartment to put some more of her belongings away, Kinshasa placed her money on top of the bill. She arose from the table and took a last curious look at the diner who had smiled at her earlier. She saw that the woman was frankly staring at her, as if they knew each other. Kinshasa looked away quickly, hoping to discourage any further eye contact. She was certain that she'd never met this woman before. Perhaps the stranger recognized her from the portrait on her book jackets. That was it. Kinshasa always forgot about her minor celebrity status until something like this happened.

The afternoon had taken on the look of early evening, with the sun painting the buildings a calm pink-gray. Kinshasa gave thanks for the six weeks that remained before she had to begin teaching her first course. She needed all that time to get settled into her new place, to plan and prepare materials, to meet her co-workers, and get the lay of the land of Allerton's English Department. And she would use that time, also, to continue forgetting Michael and the feelings that still threatened to rob her of any joy that she could possibly ever feel again.

TWO

I had one eye on the dirty coffee mug in the sink, and the other eye checking out my favorite morning news broadcaster when I noticed them. I squinted, leaned over the water splashed counter, and got my shirt wet as I pushed my nose against the window.

"The first ones! It's about time!" There wasn't a soul in my kitchen but me, but I was so happy to see those flowers, I just had to shout. And I had to be *real* happy any time I let myself be distracted from my daily visual fix of the former basketball player/commentator turned news reader. That woman had become my breakfast companion. I couldn't get into my day without knowing what part of the world she was in, what brilliantly colored outfit she was wearing, and what sharp necklace was clinging provocatively to her coffee and cream hued throat. I barely heard the news she reported, because I was too distracted looking at her. So, just imagine how important those flowers were to me.

Deep yellow and purple crocuses aimed up toward the morning sky. The past three and a half months of winter had been brutal, so I took those flowers as a sign. I threw on my jacket and rushed outside to the backyard. The cold wind was still in charge, though, having its way with the March sun and reminding me of how the bitter cold can cut right through you, no matter how anxious you are for the Spring to arrive.

I bent down and pulled away some dead leaves and shredded newspaper that had blown on top of the perennial bed, making it hard for the crocuses to break through the earth.

"I've got to help you out or you won't get a chance to bloom with all this trash on top of you."

I hoped none of my neighbors was watching. I didn't usually talk to flowers, and I didn't think that I was old enough to be labeled eccentric. My best friend, Simone, on the other hand, would find holding a conversation with plants, trees, birds or flowers very acceptable. She would encourage me, in fact. She'd say it was like verbal fertilizer. But that's Simone. She has a way of being able to suspend reality more easily than I can.

I thought about going into the garage and grabbing a rake to clear out all the trash left by the worst winter anyone can remember. December through February had been so bad that many of my neighbors were still in shock. How else could you explain the Christmas wreaths and pine roping that were still hanging from various houses on my block? And the signs of a lingering winter weren't only in my neighborhood.

Everywhere I drove I saw the evidence of the "blizzard mind blow". That's how I referred to Allerton's collective reaction to the pounding of storm after storm that we had endured that winter. For a while, I was convinced that we were living in a Stephen King novel. I'm a pretty upbeat person. But months of snow shoveling, ice scraping and cursing every time I had to drive down a hill, left me totally oppressed by nature.

So that's why this morning's appearance of color coming out of the ground was a great wake up call. The tenacity of these little flowers reminded me that I, too, had survived a horrendous fall and winter. There were times when I wasn't sure that I'd make it with mind, body and soul intact.

It was late last summer, during one of those heat wave breaking thunder storms, that Jen confessed she was having an affair with Pat. She told me that after five years of being us, she had fallen out of love with me and into love with a cop named Patricia Adamson.

It wasn't as if I'd been shocked by Jen's admission. I could feel a growing indifference when we kissed, a certain impatience. Jen had taken on this hard edged tone whenever she answered me. And we would argue over little, trivial things. So I wasn't totally surprised when she admitted her unfaithfulness. I wasn't shocked. But I did feel a long, drawn out ache. Jen had become bored with us. But I hadn't.

By now, the months of anger have melted into a mound of acceptance; the ache has numbed. The only things left here, after five years of loving each other and four of living together, are some of Jennifer's belongings. A stack of books, CD's and diskettes are hardly a shrine to our relationship. But their presence reminds me, silently, of a hurtful time, not the loving one. And they reinforce my resolve to stay clear of any serious romantic entanglements for a long while. I could go out with somebody, casually. I could even get into the sex. I miss feeling a woman's body touching mine. But I want no commitments. Not now. Not for a long while. I prefer a lake of calm and tranquility compared to the muddy waters of deceipt. It took a while, but I can enjoy doing things by myself without feeling lonely and abandoned.

So, I was glad to see those little flowers, but I was not energetic enough to rake and clean out the beds. I decided to let that go until another time. Right now, I had a lot of work waiting for me on my desk. And since I had to be on campus tomorrow, I didn't plan to work the entire day. I'd finally rented that Cheryl Dunye film that Simone had raved about. It would be great if I could carve out enough time to see it.

THREE

On the spur of the moment, I decided to celebrate my blooming crocuses by going out to an early dinner. So I headed to the Luna Negra, all by my lonesome. Eating alone in a restaurant and feeling okay with it had taken some practice, but I could do it with relative ease when my friends had other commitments and I was bored with my own cooking. Simone and Karin were still away in Massachusetts, and I didn't feel like being bothered with another friend, Charlene, and her high voltage self. Besides, I'd heard that she was cultivating a new relationship with some hot young thing. So this afternoon, I'd treat myself to my own company.

The Luna Negra is one of my favorite restaurants. It's a friendly, casual spot with good food. And I usually see other single men and women dining alone, so I feel comfortable, not so out of place. I know the owners . . . three women who have been business partners for years. One of them, Sonia Berceo, is from time to time, the subject of some of my best fantasies. Sonia, with those wonderful green eyes framed by that lovely tan face full of the earthiness of her native Portugal. Although I daydream about her, I often wonder if I'd know what to do if she ever paid any attention to me. After five years of monogamy I can hardly remember how to flirt. But . . . thinking about the possibilities of flirting with Sonia is always fun.

"Hello, Corey. Table for one?" Sonia flashed me her welcoming smile.

"Thanks, Sonia. How are you?" I tried to be as smooth as possible.

"Very busy, but grateful that business has been so good." Sonia led me towards the middle of the room, and I could see that, despite the early hour, a lot of the tables were filled.

"I guess you're lucky that business has been so brisk, considering how awful the winter was."

"You're right. It's picked up lately. But, *you* are the lucky one. The semester has ended, hasn't it?"

"Yes, but that's only temporary for me. I'm going to teach during both of the summer sessions." I felt pleased that Sonia kept up with the University schedule, my schedule. Maybe there was hope yet.

"Aren't *you* the ambitious one."

We stopped at a table. "Will this be all right?"

I nodded yes and Sonia continued to smile.

"Well, enjoy your vacation, even if it is a short one." She started to turn away, and then added, "It's always nice to see you, Corey."

I watched Sonia's retreating figure as she went back to her post near the restaurant's entrance and wished that I'd been able to make more conversation with her. But where would I have gone with it? Would I have asked her that tired old line about what time she gets off? And if she had answered "Every time I have a chance", what would I have done with that? I figured that Sonia could be quite a heart breaker. Of course, I'll never find that out first hand. Once has been enough for me. I have no intention of jumping back into *that* game.

I took a quick look at the menu, already knowing what I wanted. After I ordered, I looked around and saw that most of the diners were coupled. There were only three customers sitting by themselves, two single men and a woman who was studying the menu. She had a professional air about her, and appeared to be in her late thirties or early forties. Quite attractive. As she put her menu down, she caught me looking at her. I smiled, acknowledging our shared ethnicity. I always appreciated this relaxed recognition, and I found myself continuing to look in her direction.

She seemed somehow familiar to me, but I couldn't connect her with a name. Did I know her from the university? Maybe not. I thought that I knew all of the female African-American instructors.

There weren't that many of us. Maybe she was some professor's wife, or perhaps a member of the support staff.

I waited for my dinner to arrive and replaced trying to identify the mystery diner with watching a young guy flirt with a waiter right in front of his dinner companion. Gay boys will be gay boys. They can be so outrageous.

"What did you order?" Sonia startled me with her question. I'd been given another chance to overwhelm her with my clever repartee.

"The salmon." That was a witty answer.

"Excellent choice. Let me know if there's anything I can get for you."

I prayed for the courage to say what was on my mind. Why can't *I* be more outrageous?

After two bites of my dinner, I noticed that the mystery diner was sipping some coffee and the two male diners were now embroiled in an argument. Maybe "dinner companion" had noticed his friend's behavior with the waiter and didn't go for the flirting after all. Dinner and a side show. This was more than I'd expected. While I could do without witnessing a domestic disagreement, I was a little disappointed that the attractive stranger had finished her meal so quickly. I had been enjoying looking at her. She was a distraction from my plotting about Sonia. I wondered who she was and why she looked familiar to . . .

"Oh, Jesus." I spoke aloud to no one but myself for the second time in one day. Sonia was leading Jennifer and her lover, Pat, to a table not far from mine. This isn't the first or even the second time that I've seen them in a public place. After all, Allerton is a small town with a limited number of social and cultural resources; fewer than that for gay men and women. So I know that I could run into them at any time and anywhere. But the element of surprise is what grabs me in the gut sometimes. Basically, I feel at peace with my situation, and I've accepted their relationship. It just bugs me when I'm reminded that their relationship started on *my* time and in the middle of *my* relationship.

I'll just finish my dinner, stay calm, have a cup of coffee and take my time paying the bill. I know I'll have to pass by their table in order to get to the door, but I'm determined to be pleasant. Almost a year has passed since we split, and I'm well on my way to healing. Jennifer is part of my past. I'm determined to take care of myself in the future.

FOUR

J took the long route home from the restaurant, driving through nearby neighborhoods and wondering how long it would take some people to repair the winter's damage to their properties. It was nearly dark when I pulled into my driveway. I could hear the phone ringing as I opened the backdoor.

"Hello?"

"Hi, Corey!"

I recognized Simone's voice. "Hey, Simone! How are you?"

"I'm great! But you sound out of breath."

"I was just coming in when I heard the phone. I'm glad to hear from you. I started to let the answering machine pick up the call," I caught my breath, "but now I'm glad that I didn't."

Simone snickered. "Well, I'm glad that you made the extra effort."

"Yeah. How was P-town? How's Karin?"

"We enjoyed ourselves, girl. I really needed some time away, even if it was only for a few days."

"I'll bet it was cold up there." Before Simone could answer, I got lost in my own reverie of the dunes, the sea and the beach . . . memories of the gloriously gay P-town beach.

"Girl, it was freezing most of the time, and it was windy. We tried to walk on the beach one day, but we gave up. We were getting windburned."

"But the nice thing about being cold in P-town is the weather gives you an excuse to get close to your honey." I cast out a teasing comment to my friend.

"You're right. But Karin and I didn't need much of an excuse to snuggle."

"Oh, you poor things. You must have been bored to tears."

"Hardly!" Then, shifting gears, "Corey, do you remember the two women we met up there last year, Terez and Jasmine?"

"Sure I do." I rolodexed memories of those two. Jasmine . . . compact, serious and sincere. Terez . . . tall and outrageously flirtatious. Jennifer had taunted me cruelly by suggesting that she would have no trouble leaving me and stealing Terez from Jasmine. Of course, Jennifer hadn't checked out her plan with Terez. Nor had she met Patricia Adamson yet. That happened a couple of weeks after we returned home from the Cape. I should have been able to figure out that if Jennifer were willing to entertain the possibility of having an affair with Terez, she was ready to look around for somebody new.

Simone continued. "We ran into them our first night. They were up there looking for a summer rental. So we made a date to meet them for dinner the next night."

"That's nice." I hesitated. "Did they ask you about Jennifer and me?" I figured that they had. How could Jasmine have forgotten Jennifer's throwing herself at Terez?

"They did. But I kept my big mouth shut. I know how much you like your privacy." Simone paused and gave me a chance to respond.

"You're right about that. If I get to P-town this summer, I'll look for them." I wasn't planning a trip, but then you never know. "I'm really glad that you called, Simone. What are you and Karin up to in the next couple of weeks before the first summer session starts?"

"As little work as possible, and a lot of play. You know what I'm saying?" Simone breathed into the phone suggestively.

"Sort of. But my amnesia keeps kicking in."

Simone ignored my answer. "And what about you, my little workaholic? How are you planning to spend the next six weeks?"

"Oh, I have some house projects . . . caulking windows, a little painting, furniture refinishing, gardening. And I need to prep some of the materials I'll be using in that essay topics course."

Simone listened to me carefully. "You have a lot planned, and it all sounds like hard work. You have any playtime in mind?"

"Well, Dr. George told me that the class would be filled. And I know that once we get started I won't have a hell of a lot of time to do much pre-reading. I'll be too busy keeping up with the students' writing." I continued listing my plans. "And did I tell you that I want to sit in on some of Kinshasa Jordan's creative writing seminars?"

Simone's nonjudgmental listening jammed to a halt. "Corey! You must be crazy! The summer is your chance to slow down a little. Weren't you just complaining about being so tired after you finished grading all of your finals?"

"I know. Hey, I've started my recovery. I haven't been on campus for five days."

"I thought you told me that you were going to teach one course, and that was it for the summer." There was as much concern in Simone's voice as there was disbelief in what I was telling her.

"Yeah, I know what I said, Simone. But you don't often get a chance to sit in on a class or two with a writer of Jordan's caliber." I tried to justify my plans to my best friend.

"I know this, but you don't need to shorten your life span by working twenty-four hours a day, eleven months of the year either." Simone paused, listened to my silence and then asked, "How is everything else? Are things getting any easier for you?"

"Yes, they are. Really." Then I thought about the last couple of hours. "I had an interesting experience this afternoon."

"What happened?"

"I was hungry, so I decided to go to the Luna Negra for an early dinner. The good part of the story is that I saw Sonia Berceo."

Simone cut in. "That fine looking woman with the bedroom eyes?"

"The one and only. Anyway, the down part of the story is that, right near the end of my meal, who do I see walking in but Jennifer?"

"Was she alone?"

"Of course not. Pat was with her. They didn't see me at first, so I had time to make sure that I was together."

"Did you all speak to each other?"

"Yes. They looked up and spoke to me as I walked by their table on my way out of the restaurant. We were all very cool and sophisticated . . . like we'd been divorced for ten years, sent the kids through college and had each remarried."

"Only, you haven't." Simone interrupted.

"And I don't intend to. You know what, Simone? If you didn't know the score, you'd think that the three of us were good friends."

Simone feigned a British accent. "How veddy civilized, my dear."

"I am truly over all of that drama, girl."

"That sounds good, Corey. You know that Karin and I are sorry that it didn't work out for you and Jen. You sure did try. Maybe it just wasn't meant to be."

"Maybe not, but I could have done without all the agitation. As Kate Clinton says,'No pain . . . no pain.'"

Simone laughed. "On to another subject. Are you going to the staff meeting next week?"

"Do I have a choice?"

"No, you don't. Do you want to bet that Dr. George is going to ask you or me to organize a reception for Kinshasa Jordan?"

I nodded into the receiver. "Amazing, isn't? With six English instructors on campus this summer, it has to be one of us to get something together. Why doesn't one of the deans do it, anyway? That would be more appropriate."

"Because, love, the deans are either away for the summer, or they can't be bothered." Simone understood the politics of being a black instructor in a white university. Her survival demanded her knowing the ins and outs of Allerton.

"You're probably right. But you'd think that one of the deans would want to host a tea or something. After all, Kinshasa Jordan is trendy now. The only toes she's stepped on belong to black men."

Simone countered. "Corey, you keep forgetting where you are. It's 2005, and we're here at Allerton University. The two of us, three black male PhD's., and a latina professor doing post-doc work. The six of us are damn good teachers, *and* we provide public relations window dressing. We're all polite, well bred. Not one of us is a radical. We fit here. We allow the rest of the faculty to feel satisfied and comfortable."

"And what about the fact that you and I are lesbians?"

"That's easy to explain. Lesbians don't really exist for most of these people. We're a social and political construct. We just *think* we're attracted to women because the pool of eligible black men is so limited, what with HIV/AIDS, drugs, jail and brothers on the down low." Simone completed her diatribe, punctuating it with a smug "Understand?"

"Simone, you've got an explanation for everything."

"This is true. I'd rather have my explanations than be forced to accept somene else's." Simone laughed at her own cynicism. "Hey, Corey! Don't you think that Jordan's writing is womanist, maybe even a little on the lavender side?"

"Some of her characters could be, I guess." I remembered thinking that when I read her first novel.

I quickly thought about her plots and her characters. "That thought has occurred to me, especially after I saw her photo in the book review section of the Sunday . . ." I stopped in mid sentence. "Oh, my God, Simone. Now I know who I saw today at the Luna Negra."

"Other than Jennifer and Pat?"

"Yeah. I saw this very good looking woman sitting alone at a table. I couldn't place her, but she looked so familiar to me. It was Kinshasa Jordan!"

Simone laughed. "So it's true. You haven't been struck blind. There's hope for you yet, girl."

I chose to ignore my friend's comment. "Of course. It was Kinshasa Jordan."

I held the name Kinshasa on my tongue, and remembered one of my French teachers from my undergraduate days. Madame Bernard was an amazingly animated woman from the Cameroon in West Africa. She was so fond of talking about "le Congo before it became Zaire." Madame Bernard would breathe, "Le Congo was divided by la France and Belgique. The old capitals were Brazzaville and Kinshasa." The latter she would pronounce "Keen-sha-za."

Simone jumped into my daydream with both feet. "It probably was Jordan that you saw. I heard that she was supposed to arrive a couple of days ago. Did you say she's beautiful?"

"Simone. What I said was 'very good looking'." I wouldn't fall for my friend's bait.

"But back to her writing. She's definitely a feminist. That comes across loud and clear. Sometimes, though, I think I hear a homophobic note. She didn't give that character . . . What was his name? Raymond? She didn't paint him sympathetically at all."

Simone agreed. "And this is not the time to create a psychopathic gay character. Have you noticed that she's never written about lesbians in any of her novels?"

"And you think there's a reason for that?"

"Could be. She could be gay, you know, and very closeted."

"For some reason, I don't think so."

"If she's in the closet, it's safer for her not to write about gay women. That way she destroys all chances of guilt by association."

"We'll be meeting her soon enough. And if I know you, my dear Simone, your gaydar will be on full alert."

"As if yours won't be, Corey Lomax?"

"Mine is out of order right now."

"Right. Like you didn't enjoy seeing Sonia at the restaurant, and you haven't noticed how fine Kinshasa Jordan looks in her photos, and, it would appear, in the flesh." Simone could be tenacious.

"Looking is a far cry from doing anything about either one of them." I wanted to sound resolute.

"Okay. I hear you. You're the best judge of what's good for you." Simone yawned. "I've got to go now. Why don't we have a drink together next week after the department meeting?"

"That sounds great. Thanks for calling, Simone. And hug Karin for me."

"I will. And you try to relax a little. You'll be back on the teacher's side of the desk again before you know it."

FIVE

Kinshasa took her time walking back from the Luna Negra. As she walked, she made a mental list of jobs she needed to accomplish the next day . . . arrange delivery of the local newspaper and the "Sunday New York Times", finish unpacking the boxes that were left in the hallway, call Mr. Bardwell, the landlord, about getting her name put on her mailbox and added to the residents' directory in the vestibule. And she wanted to stop at the university to see what her office looked like.

Kinshasa stepped into the foyer and out of her shoes. She went to the kitchen, poured herself a glass of wine and dialed her friend, Gayle's, phone number.

Gayle and Kinshasa had been friends for the past twenty years, ever since they were in college together at Bryant University in central Maine. They were polar opposites but spiritual twins. Kinshasa was compact, curved, quiet. Gayle was long, angular and outgoing. She had sought out the unobtrusive Kinshasa, needing her serenity and quiet reassurance that life would be okay for her, a black girl plucked from a small semi-segregated South Carolina town and replanted in a practically all-white northeastern college.

In later years, after a layer of mutual trust had fused their friendship, Kinshasa assured Gayle that she had been just as intimidated as Gayle had been in their new surroundings. Fearful, despite her upstate New York childhood and integrated academic high school, Kinshasa had been surprised to discover that her quiet caution had been mistaken for confidence.

The two of them grew into womanhood together. Kinshasa's career took her to Chicago where she completed an internship in teaching. She missed the East coast, though. So she blew out of the Mid-west and landed in New Haven, Connecticut, where she got a teaching position in a public high school. Writing fiction and teaching "her kids" fulfilled her. Gayle's academic circuit included New York University, Howard University and now, Hofstra out on Long Island. Having earned her doctorate, and published the requisite articles at regular intervals, she was content and satisfied with herself.

Kinshasa listened as Gayle's phone rang four times. The last bell melted into her friend's taped voice. She waited for the tone, then began leaving her message.

"Gayle, this is Kinshasa. It's Sunday evening about seven o'clock and I'm . . ."

The answering machine jerked to a halt.

"'Shasa? I'm here. Sorry about the machine. I just got in."

"Hey! I'm calling from Allerton. I arrived yesterday."

"I bet you've been real busy, huh?"

"You bet right. I've been cleaning and unpacking and putting things away. I'm still not finished. There's so much to do."

"Well, don't try to do everything in one day. I was thinking about you and wondering if you'd gotten there. What's your apartment like?"

Kinshasa looked around the kitchen.

"I like it. It'll be fine for the next sixteen months." She paused. "It has two bedrooms, a kitchen, a small dining room, a bath and a half and a good sized living room. There's even a fireplace."

Returning her friend's enthusiasm, Gayle responded, "I'll give you a little while to get settled, then I'm coming down for a visit."

"Great! I'll be glad for the company." Kinshasa reached over to blot up the wet circle her wine glass had left on the kitchen table.

Gayle added cautiously, "You haven't heard from Michael, I hope."

"Not a word. I am so relieved that I made that break. Michael doesn't know exactly where I am."

"Good move, 'Shasa. Well on to a happier note! What's your new English Department like? Have you met any of the faculty yet?"

"Not really. I've only met the chairperson, a Dr. George. And Gayle, I wasn't that impressed."

"What do you mean?"

"It's a first impression, I guess. But he seems to be a bit full of himself." Kinshasa pictured the English Department Chairperson, and she remembered their brief conversation. "After two minutes, he switched from "Ms. Jordan" to "Kinshasa this and Kinshasa that", as if I'd given him permission to be so familiar with me." Kinshasa took a long sip of her wine.

"Sounds like white male privilege to me. Why don't you catch him off balance and call him . . . what's his first name again?"

"It's Richardson, I think."

"Damn, Kinshasa. His name is ass backwards. Richardson George? What was his mama thinking about?"

Kinshasa laughed at Gayle's analysis of her new chairperson and his mother.

"So what's your teaching load like?"

"A writing seminar that starts in six weeks, two African-American literature courses in the fall and spring, and maybe another writing class next May. Compared to my usual schedule, I'm in semi-retirement.

"You deserve to have an easier year."

"There's a staff meeting next week for the summer instructors. That's why I wanted to get here as early as I did. I guess I'll meet more people then."

"Probably. 'Shasa, have you ever heard of a writer named Corey Lomax?" Gayle spoke hesitantly.

"That name sounds vaguely familiar."

Gayle went on.

"She's written some short fiction, I think. My brother mentioned her name to me when I told him that you had accepted a position at Allerton. He remembered reading that she was on the staff there. Then, he found one of her books in his store and read the bio on the jacket. Unless she's on a sabbatical, you'll have company."

Kinshasa stiffened. "What do you mean by company?"

"Just that there's another sister writer in residence. Maybe you'll turn out to be friends."

"Maybe so." Kinshasa paused before asking, "If her book was in Gerald's store, does that mean that she's a lesbian?"

"Or a gay friendly feminist."

"Well, thanks for letting me know about her. I'll be on the lookout for a Corey Lomax." Kinshasa's voice had "subject closed" wrapped around it.

"'Shasa, are you sure that Michael doesn't know where you are?"

"I'm pretty certain."

"No chance of a surprise visit?"

Kinshasa shivered involuntarily at the thought of opening her apartment door and seeing Michael standing there, angrily demanding an explanation of her move from New Haven to Allerton.

"None whatsoever. We settled everything the last time we saw each other. You know, Gayle, the longer we're apart, the surer I am that Michael and I were simply not right together."

"You sound resolute, 'Shasa."

"I'm at peace with my decision and with my move." Kinshasa fingered her glass. "And one more glass of wine will make me peaceful about everything."

Gayle laughed at Kinshasa's last remark. "It's late, and you must be tired."

"I am."

"I'm so glad that you called. The next one is on me. I'll give you a call before you get your writing course started, and I''ll want to hear all the grit. Okay?"

"I promise, Gayle."

"Stay well, 'Shasa."

"You too. 'Bye for now."

As she rested the receiver on its cradle, Kinshasa smiled to herself. She swallowed the last few sips of her wine, and let her thoughts wander to the name Corey Lomax. A writer. Corey's existence was an unknown variable that Kinshasa had not planned on when she imagined a new life for herself. That new life had included her identity, an identity not necessarily related to the one she had lived in New Haven.

SIX

Dr. Richardson George stood up and grimaced, his popping knee joint announcing itself loudly to all who cared to pay attention.

"Ah, good afternoon, everyone."

Then, gesturing toward his leg, "Too much jogging and tennis for me. My muscles are rebelling."

I was sitting at a large table across from Simone, and I shot her a look that said, " . . . tennis and jogging my ass . . . the only muscle that's rebelling is in his head."

Simone smiled back at me, understandingly. We shared the same opinion about our department chair. He was a purely political man, supportive if he believed that you would be tenured, disinterested if he didn't. He treated me with tolerant respect, probably because I've published some short fiction since I've been here at Allerton. Simone has a lock on tenure what with all of the journal articles she's had published.

I saw Simone looking at the attractive woman seated next to Dr. George. She was the same woman I'd seen at the Luna Negra. So I figured that she was, indeed, Kinshasa Jordan. I recognized, also, the meaning of the smile at play on Simone's face as she telegraphed me to take a good look at Kinshasa. I had done that already, at the restaurant.

Kinshasa was even better looking in person than she was on her book covers. She had the smoothest skin, somewhere between caramel and copper. Her eyes were framed by dark, dark lashes that curled without artificial means. She wore just a hint of color on her lips.

Dr. George continued. "Everyone looks rested, so the time off, although brief, must have been restorative." He looked around at his small summer staff. "We have a short agenda today, so I'll get started if no one objects."

Certain that no one would object, he didn't pause for as much as a breath.

"First, it is my pleasure to introduce you to our visiting writer-in-residence, Ms. Kinshasa Jordan. As you all know, Kinshasa will be with us this summer and throughout the next academic year."

Dr. George deferred to the woman seated to his left. "Kinshasa, may I present you to Allerton University's summer English Arts and Literature faculty?"

"Thank you, Dr. George." Kinshasa quickly scanned each face. "I'm happy to meet all of you, and I look forward to teaching here this year."

A chorus of "welcome" answered her as Dr. George refocused the group.

"To continue, you'll find your class lists in your mailbox. And the inventory clerk in the bookstore assured me that everything you have ordered is in. The records office reminds us of the importance of adhering to their schedule. I've given them my word that we shall. Oh, one more point. During the drop and add period, let's have as few drops as possible." George guffawed. "Let's keep that tuition rolling in and staying in." He waited for the polite chuckles that never arrived. "Are there any questions?"

As the chairman had expected, there were none.

"Then I expect we'll see each other the first week of classes, if not sooner. Anything else for the good of the cause?"

Silence answered him.

"Then, this meeting is adjourned."

Several of the instructors gathered around Kinshasa, offering her their handshakes and assistance. I was negotiating my way through the small crowd when Dr. George derailed me.

"If you have a minute, Corey." He cleared his throat. "I hate to impose upon you. It's almost time for the first summer session, and I know that you're scheduled to teach a course, but I would like you to organize a little tea or reception of some kind for Kinshasa. Nothing grandiose. Small scale. Make it late May or early June. Maybe something outdoors if the weather is nice. The university will cover all of the expenses."

What I was thinking was, "Shit", but what I said was "I'll work on it, Dr. George. Why don't I get back to you next week after I've had a chance to plan something appropriate?"

"Great! Great! I knew that I could count on you." He beamed, certain that he had calculated the situation correctly. Surely, Corey Lomax would be anxious to host a get together for her African-American sister.

As I glided past the department chair, I spotted Simone talking to our mutual friend, Charlene Gray. I strolled over and touched Charlene's arm.

"Charlene, what's shaking?"

"Anything and everything, Corey. How's by you?"

"Okay. Busier than I had planned." I winked at Simone. "Guess who got tapped to throw a party for our visiting instructor?"

Simone grinned slowly. "I should have put money on it. Don't worry, Babe, I'll help you." She inclined her head toward Dr. George. "When does he want this to happen?"

"Late May or early June." I looked around the room, almost abesentmindedly "Did you both have a chance to meet Ms. Jordan?"

Charlene and Simone nodded in unison.

"Well, let me amble over to meet her. Then, let's get going, Simone. I'm thirsty." I tugged at Charlene's arm. "We're going out for an early happy hour. Want to join us?"

"Thanks,but not this time. I have other fish to fry." Charlene was grinning broadly like the proverbial Cheshire cat.

Simone tugged on my arm.

"Go on and introduce yourself to Kinshasa, Corey. I'll wait here for you. I want to find out what our friend Charlene has been up to. And Corey? Remember our telephone conversation last Sunday? I'll bet you anything that Ms. Jordan goes to our church. Go meet her, and then tell me if I'm not right."

I walked away from Simone and pitched her a "You crack me up", over my shoulder.

Kinshasa, now abandoned by her new colleagues, was walking toward the door when I intercepted her.

"Excuse me, Ms. Jordan. If you have one more second, I wanted to introduce myself to you. I'm Corey Lomax." I extended my hand.

Kinshasa responded with a warm, firm grip. "It's nice to meet you, Dr. Lomax."

She tried to figure out where she had seen Corey before. Then she remembered the Luna Negra restaurant and the woman who had smiled at her as she ate her dinner. She remembered her talk with Gayle, also.

"I understand that you're a writer also."

I grasped Kinshasa Jordan's hand, mindful of how firmly she held mine and looked into her eyes, directly but I hoped, not rudely. I hadn't been close enough to her at the restaurant to notice their serenity.

"I'm flattered that you know that. Actually, I've been planning to sit in on some of your seminar sessions this summer, if you don't mind."

I hoped that I wasn't being too intense. I realized that I'd been talking quickly, focusing on expressing myself correctly, and not on the bet with Simone.

"That's fine with me. Now I'm the one who is flattered."

Kinshasa did a quick study of Corey, and decided that she liked her straightforward manner. "Feel free to sit in whenever you'd like."

"Thanks." I wanted to prolong the conversation. "Have you gotten settled in to university housing?"

"I'm in the process of getting settled, but not in to university housing. I've rented an apartment on Rosedale Terrace, not far from the campus."

I nodded. "That's a pretty part of town. I used to live near there." Almost at a loss for words I added, "Listen, I'll be in my office tomorrow morning. So if you have any questions or need any information, don't hesitate to ask."

"Thank you. Everyone's been so helpful."

Caught up in Kinshasa's gaze, I suddenly remembered something more to say. "I almost forgot to mention how much I've enjoyed your novels. In fact, I've used excerpts from you second one in my topics and composition classes."

"That's gratifying." Kinshasa smiled slightly and took a step back as she once again offered her hand to Corey. "It's been a pleasure meeting you, Dr. Lomax."

"Please call me Corey. I'll see you soon."

While Kinshasa walked away, I got Simone's attention and pointed to the door. We left the department office along with Charlene . . . two women headed for drinks and the third headed to her fish fry.

SEVEN

Elbow deep in books and rough drafts of my syllabus, I reached over my glass of lemonade and picked up the ringing telephone.

"Well, dear Corey, what do you think? Is she or isn't she?" Simone's voice danced through the phone wires.

I knew what she was talking about, but I didn't want to make it easy for her. "Is who or isn't who *what*, Simone?"

"Our new writer-in-residence. Don't you pick her up on your gaydar screen?"

"Not particularly." I took a sip from my glass. "Didn't we already have this conversation over drinks the other afternoon?"

"Yeah. We did. But you didn't see things my way, and I'm persistent."

"I can tell."

"Why don't you think she's gay?"

"Just what about her *seems* gay to you, Simone?"

"I can sense it. I think she's closeted, afraid her books won't sell if the public knows the truth about her private life."

"You know what? You should be the short fiction writer, not me." I rattled the ice cubes against the sides of my glass, absentmindedly.

"Corey Lomax! Are you brain dead or what?"

"My brain works fine. It's everything else that's numb."

"I don't believe you, sister. You're lying."

"If I'm lying I'm flying." I had to laugh at my response to an increasingly frustrated Simone.

"You think that she's gay, don't you? You just don't want to admit it. And, you think she's attractive, don't you?" Simone paused expectantly.

Now I was feeling frustrated with Simone's tenacity. "Simone, how did you get *there* from *here*? You're acting like a high school girl gossiping about a new teacher."

"That's it! You're just pretending that you think she's straight!" What confidence Simone crowed!

"Don't become a detective, all right Simone? You lack the talent."

"I have your number, Corey Lomax."

"Simone?"

"Corey?"

"I'm not interested in anything about Kinshasa Jordan except her talent for writing. I don't care if she's straight or gay or in between. I don't have the time for that right now. And, besides, it takes too much energy."

"Okay. I hear you. But, at least admit one thing, Corey. You find her attractive."

"I hadn't thought about it, Simone. We're all here to teach . . . to work at Allerton. We're just colleagues."

"Okay, Corey. I'll get off your case. For now, anyway."

EIGHT

Jennifer Renfrew kicked the sheets from her legs and reluctantly rolled her way to a standing position. Walking toward the bathroom, she spotted steam seeping between the bottom of the door and the marble threshold. Pat was already in the shower. Jennifer entered the bathroom and examined her face in the mirror. The moisture distorted her image, making it ghostlike. But she could still discern the lines that appeared where smooth, taut skin had once prevailed. Dark brown strands of hair intermingled with newly gray ones.

Pat saw the blurred outline of her lover through the glassblock shower wall. "Jen, you're awake."

"I'm getting there slowly."

"Come into the shower with me."

"Not this morning, Hon. I've got cramps something fierce. Must be those damned fibroids. I'm going to make some tea so that I can take an aspirin. I'll shower in a while."

Jennifer snatched her bathrobe from its hook on the bathroom door. One arm in, and the other out, she headed for the kitchen. The cool tile beneath her feet felt good. She filled the kettle with tap water and turned the stove's burner to high. As she massaged her stomach, she looked at the calendar on the side of the fridge. She had three appointments today, two of them before noon. The pace in the admissions office hadn't slowed down much, despite the fast approach of summer. At least, she and Pat would be able to get away in July. That is, barring any unforeseen problem, like a riot in Philly or a sudden spike in the number of rapes. Pat, a detective in the Special Victims Unit of the Philadelphia Police Department, had been able to nail down a block of consecutive vacation days. They planned to drive to Portland, Maine, and from there take a ferry to Nova Scotia.

Jennifer gulped a mouthful of tea and swallowed an aspirin with a dose of guilt as she recalled that last April she and Corey had talked about going to Halifax and Peggy's Cove for their next vacation. Corey was the planner, always plotting the future. But neither Corey nor Jen had planned on the impact that Detective Patricia Adamson would make when she interviewed Jennifer about the abduction and rape in the city, of an Allerton University Admissions Office employee.

Detective Adamson's blunt, frank gaze traveled right through Jennifer at the same time that she and Corey were in rough waters. After the initial interview, Jennifer could hardly wait to use the phone number imprinted on Pat's business card. It was true that later that day Jennifer had remembered previously forgotten details about the victim's workday before she was dragged from her car and driven to Philadelphia. But Jennifer's memory surged in tempo with a very sudden urge to know the detective better. She hadn't set out to hurt Corey, nor to kill their relationship, when she suggested that she meet Pat at a women's bar in the city, and not at the police station. She simply gave Corey and their relationship no thought at all.

It was Jennifer who followed Pat to Pat's apartment later that afternoon . . . after a few drinks and lingering looks. It was Jennifer who refused to block out the erotic memory of Pat's lovemaking. It was Pat, who, after two months of secret meetings, said that she would feel more honest if they could stop deceiving Corey. And it was Pat, Jennifer and Corey who bounced back and forth in a tangle of guilt, accusations, anger and bitterness as Jennifer cut the five year old ties that had bound her to Corey.

Jennifer was certain that Corey would get over it. She had her work, her friends, her writing, her house. They could run into each other now on campus and know that the wounds they had inflicted upon each other were not fatal.

Pat's voice pulled Jennifer back from her daydreams.

"Jen, Honey, I'm running late." Pat slipped her service revolver in place, put on her jacket and picked up a black leather portfolio. "Do me a favor, and pour some of that hot water into the thermos. The instant coffee's already in."

Jennifer complied. Twisting the cap on snugly, she handed Pat her coffee along with a lascivious appraisal.

"I think I know what's on your mind, but you missed your chance when you didn't get into the shower with me."

"I knew that turning you down was dicey, but what could I do under the circumstances?"

Pat chuckled. Then she reached for the collar on Jen's robe and pulled her close. "I could get very attached to you, woman."

"I feel that way about you, too, Detective. Be careful with any interviews that you might do today. You know where they can lead."

Pat kissed Jennifer gently, and then left the apartment.

Jennifer showered, got dressed and considered calling Corey to set up a lunchtime meeting. They both needed to decide when Jennifer could finally collect the rest of her belongings from Corey's house. She picked up the receiver, dialed Corey's number, but at the last moment, put the phone down. She felt less guilty about Corey these days, but she knew damn well that there were still moments when she missed her. She missed sharing the latest university gossip . . . missed their conversations about films and books, missed the heat of their early intimacies.

NINE

Pat plunked her thermos down and saw the stack of new files waiting for her attention. The one on the bottom sat smack on top of the "ke" of "dyke" that someone had so thoughtfully carved into her desk a couple years ago. She smiled as she remembered her rebellious mood the day she first saw the graffiti. Instead of trying to mask it or sand it away, she took a pen and darkened the letters, making them even more prominent. Everyone, from her captain to the pizza delivery person, had seen that tag.

"It gets all the shit out into the open real fast." Pat once explained to Jennifer. "No games, no mind fucks, no shame. Life is too short."

Pat took a deep breath, opened the first file and removed two photos. The little bit of coffee she'd had time to drink threatened to surge back up from her stomach.

"Jesus Christ!" She thought she was hardened to everything the Special Victims Unit had to offer an investigating officer. But each week there was one more atrocity, one more twist in a never ending circle of horrors.

"Morning, Pat." Captain Jenson looked down at her.

"I'm glad that you didn't put a 'good' in front of that 'morning'."

Jenson allowed himself a quick smile, and then nodded toward the folder in Pat's hand.

"That's a pretty bad one. It came in after you left yesterday. Take a minute to read the preliminary report. Detective Jones started working on it, but she wants your help. So take a few minutes to bring yourself up to speed. D.H.S. is involved. They have a running history on the family. The victim is in St. Christopher's Hospital."

"You mean she's still alive?"

"Yeah. She survived. I want you and Jones to pay a call on the suspected perp. Make that a.s.a.p. Jones is due here within the hour."

An hour is not enough, Pat thought, as she plowed through the report. The victim was an eight year old named Elisa Rodriquez. She was a third grade student at St. John the Divine Elementary School in the Fairhill section of the city. The Department of Human Services had a case file on the family as long as the child was tall. Teachers, counselors, neighbors . . . It seemed as if everyone had called something in at one time or another. A lot of people had tried to save that little girl.

Pat picked up the photos to take a second look. The body shot showed a ragdoll of a child, left leg contorted, right forearm fractured, the bone pushing through the skin. Her genital area was a combination of black, blue and red.

The second picture, the one of Elisa's face, was even worse. Her bluish lips ballooned away from broken off teeth. Her nose was flattened. There was caked blood where her forehead met her hairline. Her eyes were puffed shut. Pat had seen such photos before, but they were always of corpses. She'd never had to interview anyone who looked like this. People don't usually survive this kind of abuse. A face and body this badly damaged usually give up their soul to death.

"Hey, Pat. Sorry I'm running late this morning."

Detective Johnetta Jones sat down across from Pat. "You've seen the file, huh?"

"Yeah. Not the best way to start the morning."

"Not a good way to end the day, either. Trust me." Johnetta leaned back in her chair and pursed her lips. "So, are you ready to go out and pick up the m.f.?"

"You bet. Do we have a warrant?"

Johnetta patted her jacket pocket. "Right here."

Pat openly admired her partner and had told her so more than a few times. Johnetta was smart, sensitive, efficient. Like Pat, she was up front. She lived and breathed the fight against discrimination at the police academy and on the job.

They had worked together only a few days when Johnetta watched Pat filling in the etched "dyke" on her worn desk. Johnetta had just smiled and asked, "Tell me, partner, do you have a good woman in your life?"

Pat had laughed and answered, "Johnetta, this is the beginning of a beautiful working relationship."

Johnetta drove the unmarked car through the streets of Fairhill. She radioed for backup, in case the suspect had running away in mind.

"The perp is the girl's brother. He's nineteen, has a record a yard long . . . burglaries, b. and e's., one assault and a charge of raping a former girlfriend. Brutalizing his sister must be his new hobby. I guess he thought his repertoire was getting old."

They pulled up in front of a narrow row house.

"Is this the address, Johnnie?"

"Yeah. An anonymous caller phoned 911 yesterday afternoon. Gave him up and said we could find him here. The dumb shit came right back home. We found the little girl in the alley out back."

The two detectives got out of the car. Pat unsnapped her holster and simultaneously looked up toward the roofs of the neighboring houses. Johnetta was the first to reach the top step. She pounded on the door.

"Israel Pagan! It's the police! Open the door!"

They heard the screech of old wood straining against a window frame. Instinctively, Pat and Johnetta slammed their backs against the brick front of the house. Big chunks of cinderblock rained down in front of them.

"Shit! Now I'm mad." Johnetta gripped her nightstick. "We're going in, Pat!"

Johnetta was poised to kick open the door. "That back up better get here quick!"

Her foot shattered the flimsy rotted wood. The door splintered. Pat crouched behind her as they entered the front room of the house.

"Johnnie, left!" Pat yelled the second that she saw the glint of a heavy chain, made bright by the sunshine cutting through what had been the door.

Johnetta pushed the chain wielding man into a table. Pat drew her revolver, removed the safety and hissed, "If you even think about using that chain, it'll be your last thought." She grasped her gun with both hands and aimed the barrel at the man's chest.

"Israel Pagan?" Johnetta snapped

"Yeah?"

"You're under arrest. You have the right to remain silent . . ."

"Mierda!" Pagan spit at Pat's feet. "Ain't no mariconas gonna arrest me! Bullshit!"

"Wrong! It's not mierda! It's Miranda. Now shut your ass up, and I'll start all over again." Johnetta didn't even recognize shit, much less take any from some hoodlum.

Two uniformed cops stormed in. "Everything under control?"

"You two, cuff Mr.Pagan, mirandize him and give him a limo ride back to the station."

Pat caught Johnetta's eye and motioned to the staircase leading to the second floor. They climbed the steps cautiously. As soon as they reached the top, they heard a low, whimpering sound coming from the bedroom in the back of the house. Its door was ajar. Pat nudged it fully open, and went in with her gun drawn. Johnetta had her back to Pat's. She kept looking down the dark hallway. She could feel Pat's back relax slightly, and then she heard her partner's command.

"Get up from the bed and hold your arms out! We want to see your hands!"

Johnetta turned around. She and Pat looked at a middle aged woman with a tear streaked face. She wore a torn half slip, a bra and no shoes. Her outstretched arms bore purple bruises.

"What's your name? Como se llama usted?" Pat broke the silence.

"Ana Rodriguez." The woman began to shake and whimper.

"Are you the mother of Elisa Rodriguez?"

"Yes. Si."

"Where are your clothes? In that closet over there?" Johnetta's tone softened. "You have to get dressed Mrs. Rodriguez. You have to come with us."

"Are you arresting me?"

"No. We want to talk with you, to ask you some questions."

Pat walked over to the closet and opened its door.

"Did you arrest Issi? Did you hurt my Issi?" The woman was agitated.

"You mean Israel? The kid that came at us with the chain?" Johnetta's softness disappeared. "He tried to assault police officers."

"But he didn't mean it. He was afraid." The woman moved toward a chest of drawers and began taking clothes out of it.

"Afraid of what, Ma'am?" Pat saw an opening, a way of getting in formation from the woman.

"He was afraid you were coming after him about Elisa." The woman put on a blouse.

"What about Elisa, Ma'am?" Pat probed carefully.

"He didn't need to be arrested because of Elisa. I *told* him to punish her."

Pat gestured to the bed. "Why don't you sit down for a minute, Mrs. Rodriguez. Get yourself together." Pat gave her a few seconds to sit comfortably, and then she continued.

"Why did you tell Issi to punish Elisa?"

The woman's eyes flashed.

"Elisa es mala! She's evil. She was sent here by Satan. I told Issi, 'You're my son. You have to protect me from her.' I told him to break her in two. All the other times . . . they didn't work."

"The other times?" Johnetta asked as if the woman were telling a fairy tale.

"We tried to burn her with cigarros. She didn't die. She's the devil! She's from hell! We held her feet in a bucket of hot oil! But she still lived! Mala criatura!"

"Did you tell Issi to violate her? To have sex with her?" Pat struggled to keep her voice even.

"No! Nunca! That's someone else! My Issi is good. He does only what I tell him. He wouldn't do that!" The woman jumped to her feet. "Where did they take him? To jail?"

Johnetta stood at the woman's side, ready to restrain her if necessary. Pat took some clothing out of the closet.

"Here's a sweater and a pair of slacks, Ma'am. Put them on, and come with us. You'll be able to see Issi."

Johnetta lead the woman downstairs and out of the house. She and Pat drove back to the station. Once they were there, they turned the woman over to the sergeant on duty. Johnetta went out to grab a quick lunch, and Pat went into the bathroom to vomit whatever was left of her breakfast.

TEN

Charlene and I were in the Quick Print when we ran into Kinshasa. I knew very well that I should save my money and have the work-study students at the university run off copies of King's "Letter Written from a Birmingham Jail", but I was in a hurry. My time is as precious as my money, and the course starts next week. Lately, I've wasted too many minutes on my porch, drinking iced tea and lemonade, and not enough time preparing notes.

Charlene went to pick out display boards and markers while I waited my turn at the copy center. I noticed Kinshasa standing not far from me, studying the price list. She wore the same serious expression on her face that she'd had that late Sunday afternoon at the Luna Negra. There was something about the quality of her concentration that I didn't want to disturb by suddenly stepping into her space. So, I spoke softly, while still yards away.

"Ms. Jordan . . . Kinshasa . . . hello."

She looked around quickly. "Oh, hello."

"I see that you've found the fasting copy service in town."

Surveying the store, Kinshasa responded. "It looks that way. I stopped in to see what the prices are like, although Dr. George assured me that the university's copying facility is at my disposal."

I nodded, all the while noticing that I felt happy but nervous talking to Kinshasa. "They do a decent job. You just have to be sure to get your material to them in plenty of time, especially during the summer when they're short on staff."

"I thought about that. Their hours are shorter, also. In case I'm ever pushed for time, it's good to know what other resources are available. This place is so close to my apartment."

"That's smart of you." I nodded and saw that Kinshasa was looking around. I began to feel awkward, as if I were trying to force the conversation while she was looking for a way to end it.

"That woman standing near the art supplies . . . isn't she in our department?" Kinshasa inclined her head to the left, but I couldn't tell if she was talking about Charlene or the woman standing next to her.

"The white woman or the black one?" I seized the most obvious descriptors.

"The white woman with mixed gray hair."

"Oh sure, that's Charlene. You probably remember meeting her at Monday's staff meeting."

Charlene had told me that she'd introduced herself to Kinshasa. I knew her well. So I knew that she would not have missed an opportunity to meet an attractive woman.

"I thought that I'd met her, but I couldn't remember her name." Kinshasa continued to stare at Charlene. So much for *my* ability to hold her attention.

"She's Charlene Gray. She's not only a colleague, she's a friend whom I admire quite a bit."

Kinshasa looked at me, a question mark taking shape on her forehead. I went on. "Charlene was the first female to be granted tenure in Allerton's English Department. They used to have the habit of hiring women as part timers. But Charlene hung in there and became full time. Then, she applied for tenure. She's had some very interesting experiences here in the land of academia."

Although she was listening to me, Kinshasa never took her eyes off of Charlene.

"A few of us have been encouraging her to write a book, but she's a procrastinator. Maybe having a writer here on campus this year will give her the nudge that she needs to get started. You could be her motivator."

Kinshasa looked at me skeptically. "Maybe so."

Charlene saw us talking. She walked over and said how nice it was to see Kinshasa again. Kinshasa's response was tepid. I felt her turning away as Charlene and I continued to stand there. But I was too stupid with disbelief to undo the slow motion of her good-bye.

"I have to be going. I have so much to do. I'll see you back on campus." She walked away quickly.

I glanced at Charlene and decided not to say anything about Kinshasa's abrupt departure. The book was barely open on her, and life was too short to be bothered with petty criticisms of somebody's manners. Clearly, though, Charlene's ego was wounded. She couldn't resist commenting.

"Do you think I make her nervous?"

I winked at Charlene. "You make a lot of people nervous. You used to make *me* nervous many moons ago."

Charlene chuckled when I reminded her of our ages old attraction to one another.

Dr. Charlene Gray is five feet six inches of incredible intensity. Her hazel eyes unmask everyone she talks to, male or female. If you're a woman, though, Charlene invades your skin. She enchants you and makes you feel caressed in supportive arms even if she's fifty feet away. She has this way of leaning into your space, just as one voice inside your head is asking her to, and the other voice is screaming a danger warning.

During my first year at Allerton, I went into a tailspin over Charlene. What saved me, was getting close enough to see her flaws next to mine, and being able to imagine the scorching heat of her flame as it burned from one woman to the next. It didn't take a genius to see that Charlene had taken serial monogamy to a new level. What *had* been an overwhelming crush lead rather smoothly to a friendship based upon mutual respect and our similar talent for coupling with the wrong women.

"So what does it mean that our new writer-in-residence flew the coop as soon as I came along?"

"Probably that she has a lot to do." I tried my best to sound convincing.

"Corey, you're so cute when you're being naive." Charlene tapped the end of my nose.

Naiveté had little to do with my answer. It was pure b.s. I believe that Kinshasa split for a pretty obvious reason. She did not want to be around Charlene. Beneath Kinshasa's calm polite exterior lay a pool of nervousness. But why would Charlene make her tense?

I spend time looking at women. Not just "clocking" them, as my young lesbian students say; but appreciating them. I love the way some women walk, holding their heads erect, completely in charge of their body language. I admire the beauty of their eyes. I can stop my soul and rest it awhile on the face of a truly intriguing woman.

I've looked carefully at Kinshasa twice now in the space of a few days. And I've seen that she is the color of polished bronze. A mass of dark tendrils threatening to be an Afro, covers her head and trails down the course of her soft and proudly held neck. Smile-etched indentations border her mouth, which is full-lipped, but, I imagine, incomplete without a kiss. I have looked at Kinshasa a few times now, and each time that I've looked, what I've recognized in her eyes is a beauty and loneliness so poignant that it's made the deep part of me ache.

My buddy, Simone, decided right away that Kinshasa is a gay woman. Charlene agreed with her. I've dusted them both off with my doubts. I'm not ready to deal with what I've seen in Kinshasa. I can't tolerate thinking about any possibilities with our visiting professor. Why should I open myself up to any more pain? But indeed, I have looked carefully and deeply at Kinshasa Jordan.

ELEVEN

Kinshasa had seen Charlene Gray at the first department meeting. And everything about Charlene: her too-quick smile, her serious "what you are saying is the most profound idea that has ever been expressed" stare, the imposition of her body into your space, reminded Kinshasa so much of Michael. Thinking about Michael reminded her of how she had escaped the emotional death that Michael would have delivered if she had stayed in that relationship.

After seeing Charlene with Corey Lomax at the Quick Print, Kinshasa felt an active distrust of her. She remembered Michael's guile and deceptively seductive personality, and she wondered about the nature of Charlene's and Corey's relationship. Corey seemed to worship Charlene professionally. She'd said that they were good friends. Did they have a closer bond? If they did, how long would it be before Corey discovered the cruelty that undoubtedly lay beneath Charlene's charm? Would Charlene explain her infidelities with the back of her hand, as Michael had done?

Kinshasa chided herself for being overly concerned about Corey's welfare. She hardly knew her, and it wasn't any of her business. Perhaps Corey and Charlene were just co-workers and friends. Or maybe they were at the beginning of their relationship when everything is fresh. Fresh gets stale pretty quickly when you keep finding the signs of betrayal. Unexplained absences, excuses that are so poor that they are embarrassing, phone calls from a woman who knows more about your lover than you do, accusations that are slapped back across your mouth.

If she concentrated, Kinshasa could still feel the flesh of her left eyelid pulsing in pain as she recoiled from Michael's fist. The second blow slit a quarter inch gash over her cheekbone. The reality of her blood sadly drifting down her cheek had been her rescue call. Kinshasa grappled with memories that were interred with her mother.

> "No man ever hit me, Kinshasa. Your father and I might have argued and yelled the thirty years we were together, but he never once raised his hand to me. He knew better. And don't you ever live with anyone who would hit you. That's not love. You're better off dead and buried than alive and afraid."

The day that Michael's fist slammed into her eye, Kinshasa touched her face, and then screamed as her blood fell toward the floor.

Michael didn't try to contact her for weeks. The blood had been too much, even for the abuser.

TWELVE

Patricia Adamson shut her eyes tightly, determined to rest, at least, if she couldn't sleep. The dull fluorescent green of the alarm clock assured her that she had three more hours before she had to get up and face another brain battering day.

Events from the last forty-eight hours flowed through her mind in stream of consciousness rivulets . . . The eighth grader, violated and broken by her mother's boyfriend, a cretin unable to see anything wrong with raping a thirteen year old whose mother wasn't "putting out" often enough to satisfy him . . . the legal secretary dragged into a stairwell and beaten into unconsciousness after being forced to masturbate her attacker until his semen soiled her . . . the emergency room interviews . . . a high school boy pulled into the gym locker room and, taunted by a half dozen of his schoolmates determined to "beat the faggot out of him", taught lessons no one should have to learn . . . Elisa Rodriguez and her insane mother and brutal brother.

Unable to keep her eyes shut any longer, Pat reached over to the night table and retrieved her Walkman. With her headset pumping soft music into her brain, she concentrated on how to extricate herself from her present assignment without appearing to be giving up. The cumulative lack of sleep and her fast growing paranoia about her and Jennifer's safety were building a wedge between them.

Six years ago, freshly assigned to the Special Victims Unit, Pat reveled in her promotion. She had worked diligently since her first day at the police academy, and she knew that she had earned her rank. The unit had been top heavy with male officers. Pat, Johnnie and two other female detectives represented the force's attempt to be more sensitive to women. After all, women were disproportionately represented when it came to being crime victims. Competent and compassionate, Pat was a model officer. She delved into each case with a gritty drive unequaled by any of her peers. For a while, she truly loved her new assignment. One of her cases had brought Jennifer into her life.

Their beginning was not an ideal one, but their life together had evolved into the kind of relationship that Pat had craved. She truly loved, as well as was in love with Jen. Pat had all but forsaken her small condo in the city, and spent most of her off-duty time in Jen's Allerton apartment. They talked about buying a house together within the city limits, as Pat was obliged to live in Philadelphia as long as she remained a city cop. But right now, remaining a cop in the Special Victims unit felt like a jail sentence.

Jennifer moved slightly and reached out for Pat. Her hand brushed the thin metal headset, knocking it askew from Pat's ear.

"You can't sleep again?" Jennifer opened her eyes and focused on her lover's worried face. "Damn it, Pat! You've got to get out of that job. You can't keep going on like this."

"*I* can't . . . or *you* can't?"

"*We* can't. I deserve a full night's sleep, too."

Pat pulled Jennifer close and rubbed her back.

"I know, babe. I'm sorry I keep waking you up. I feel like I've got an alarm clock in my head, and it's permanently set for two-thirty a.m."

"You do have an alarm clock in your head. It runs on stress."

"This is the first time in my life that I haven't known what to do. I just can't quit the unit."

"What about that new program your captain mentioned? The one in the high school? He said you'd be perfect for it."

Pat stopped stroking Jennifer's back as she considered the possibility.

"He did say that they were going to start it at a second high school . . . Jefferson, I think. They need someone to supervise it."

"And", Jennifer added, "You said you were flattered that he asked you for advice. He said you're so calm and level-headed in a crisis." Jennifer touched Pat's cheek. "Why don't you volunteer to leave Special Victims and transfer to this new unit? That way, it won't seem like you're quitting, just changing your direction."

Pat stared at the ceiling. "I don't know, honey. I'll think about it."

She turned to face Jennifer, lowering her head until her mouth reached Jennifer's breasts. Then, she began to kiss the soft, warm contours of Jen's flesh. Awake and now aroused, Jennifer kissed the top of Pat's head and pulled her closer.

"Are we going back to sleep . . . or making love?"

"Let's do one, and then the other."

Pat banished all her work related thoughts and gathered Jennifer to her, covering her shoulders and breasts with small, quick kisses. She licked the slightly rounded plane that was Jen's stomach and filled her navel with her tongue. Jennifer abandoned sleep and wrapped her legs around Pat's thighs.

"Oh, Jen, I do love you." Pat murmured in satisfied moans. She caressed Jennifer's back and then, gently, lowered one hand toward her lover's inviting mound.

"Pat, come in to me now." Jennifer cajoled Pat's fingers deep inside of her. Her legs tightened their grip around Pat's thighs. There was no place to go, no place Pat wanted to go other than further inside of Jennifer. With her other hand she cradled Jennifer's hips, but Jen's rhythmic contractions made holding on impossible.

"Pat! Oh God! Pat!" Pat shuddered a response as Jennifer, brought to the edge, trembled and then loosened her hold on her lover. Pat's smile covered all of Jennifer, like a soft summer mist.

"Since I woke you up, the least I could do was help you get back to sleep."

Jennifer's barely audible "Thank you" got lost in her haste to return to sleep. Pat watched as she closed her eyes. "I love you, Jen. I truly do."

She glanced at the clock and sighed her determination to use the last two hours until dawn, figuring out how best to leave the Special Victims Unit. And a little bit of her wondered why Jen hadn't tried in the slightest to return the lovemaking to her.

THIRTEEN

I watched Kinshasa park her car across the street from my house, make her way up the driveway and stop to smell the sweet scented honeysuckle that grew along side the walkway. She was right on time for the Saturday afternoon reception that I had organized in her honor. I had to admit, grudgingly, that I'd enjoyed all the planning and arranging and the spending of English Department money to throw this little shindig. Simone had a field day with my enthusiasm, of course.

"Corey, I haven't seen you this excited in along time."

I ignored her.

At first, I had suggested that Kinshasa might want to read some passages from her last novel. She agreed. But during a subsequent phone call, I told her that she was off the hook. We were all working so hard, and the early June weather held mid-July's furious heat and humidity. If you've ever been near Philadelphia in the summertime, you know what I mean. There was no good reason for Kinshasa to stress herself with the pressure of having to do a public reading.

"I want you to feel comfortable, relaxed. Just get to know the staff a little." She seemed grateful for the change in plans.

I haven't had a chance to go to any of Kinshasa's seminar sessions. Actually, I *have* had the time, but I've decided against it. I'm not sure why. Simone keeps pushing me. She says that a writer can always learn something from another one. But I don't always trust Simone's motives.

When Kinshasa climbed the four steps to the front porch, I was right there, holding the door open for her.

"Kinshasa, welcome! Did you have any trouble finding your way?"

"No not at all. Your directions were great." Kinshasa smiled shyly.

I felt my cheeks grow warm as I silently admired how good Kinshasa looked in the swirling colors of her dress. Maybe I was a bit overwhelmed by her celebrity.

"Come on out to the back and see everybody." I gestured toward the back part of the house, and lead her past the living and dining rooms, to the kitchen. I was aware that she was looking around, taking everything in.

"These oak floors are beautiful." Kinshasa pointed to the freshly waxed floor planks.

"Thanks. Believe it or not, they don't take too much work. A quick polish once in a while." Why was I lying? She's not going to believe that.

"Your home is lovely."

"Thank you, again. I'll show you the rest of it a little later, if you'd like." I surprised myself with the happy jolt I felt at the thought of showing Kinshasa a part of my private world. "Let me know if the party gets boring, or if Dr. George is beating your ears to death."

We both laughed. "Did I say that?"

"Yes, you did." Kinshasa smiled conspiratorially.

"Well, if he does, I'll come by, sweep you up and take you on the grand tour." I barely got that out without stammering. Where had " . . . sweep you up . . ." come from?

Kinshasa gracefully saved me from melting into the highly polished kitchen floor. "I doubt very much, Corey, that any party you would throw could be boring. But I'll remember your offer, just in case."

We reached the back door, and I ushered Kinshasa out to the yard. I had worked like a dog on the lawn and the landscaping, and I was sorry that I couldn't take the time to show her all of the carefully mulched perennials, and explain all of their names. That would have to be another time, certainly not now.

"Our guest of honor is here, everybody." I walked beside Kinshasa long enough to reach a small knot of people, and to listen as she eased herself into the conversation. Then I slipped away to find Owen and Gary, two friends I had hired to cater the party.

Simone saw Kinshasa surveying the yard, so she strolled over to greet her. "Hi, Kinshasa. It's good to see you."

"Good to see you, too, Simone." Kinshasa pivoted and took in her surroundings. "Corey's home and yard are beautiful. I love all of these flowers."

With my welfare always uppermost in her mind, Simone answered. "Please tell her how much you like it. She works as hard out here as she does at school, or at her word processor."

Simone couldn't do a better job promoting me if I paid her.

"But sometimes I worry about her. She works too much, and she doesn't get enough playtime. She needs to do more socializing."

I could feel Kinshasa looking in my direction.

"Is she working on her next short fiction anthology?"

"I don't think that she's at the writing stage yet. She says that they're in her head though."

"I know what that's like."

Simone touched Kinshasa's arm.

"Would you like something to drink? I'll get the first one for you, then you're on your own."

"Thanks. I'd love a glass of white wine." Kinshasa liked Simone's bubbling spirit, and her obvious loyalty and concern for Corey.

"Coming right up." Simone sped to an area near the house where a bar had been set up. When she returned, she noticed that Kinshasa had been surrounded by the pomposity of Drs. Richardson George and Carter Washington. Simone hadn't expected to see Carter until the end of the summer at the university, not at this reception in Corey's backyard. But here he was, looking like a fashion model right off the pages of "Ebony Magazine" or "G.Q." Carter always seemed to be well cared for, pampered, hair and mustache impeccably groomed, trousers perfectly creased, face smoothly shaved, just the right amount of cologne.

"Carter, I thought that you were away." Simone handed Kinshasa her glass of wine.

"I am away, technically." Carter turned to Simone and bowed stiffly from the waist. He shook her hand. "I make weekend pit stops at home to check on things."

He included Kinshasa in his gaze. "I went into our office yesterday, and I saw the announcement that Corey had posted."

Simone forced a half smile and remembered that she had warned me about tacking up that notice. "You never know what fool might show up at a party that's advertised publicly." Carter proved her point.

"It said that all English Department faculty was invited. So here I am, popping up like a bad penny."

Simone considered several rejoinders, but checking out Carter's physical proximity to Kinshasa, and his leering glances, she settled for inquiring about the health of his wife and two children.

"They're fine, thanks." Always the master of discretion when discussing his family, Carter knew how to short circuit a conversation that he wanted no part of.

Kinshasa didn't miss the tone and topic of Simone's question, and she felt slightly amused that Simone had her welfare in mind. She could protect others as well as she sometimes seemed to protect her friend Corey.

Carter held out his hand.

"And you must be Kinshasa Jordan, the guest of honor. I'm Carter Washington. I'm in the English Department also."

"It's nice to meet you." Kinshasa noticed that Carter's grip was as demanding as his smile was engaging. A quick appraisal told her, though, that Carter was more impressed with himself than she would be.

Simone heard Charlene's voice in the background, and, figuring that her work was done there, excused herself. "Help yourself to more wine, or some food, Kinshasa."

Kinshasa, also, had noticed Charlene's arrival with a young woman who stood next to her. Charlene spotted Kinshasa, and smiled and waved at her. Kinshasa barely returned the smile. Instead, she tipped her wine glass to Carter and beamed up at him.

I looked over in time to see Kinshasa slay Carter with a grin and a touch on his arm. Frankly, I was annoyed that Carter was here. And I was surprised by Kinshasa's display of charm. I tried to figure out which would be the worst of two evils: that Kinshasa might truly be straight, or that she might actually find that ass-hole, Carter, interesting.

I watched them for a few seconds more. Kinshasa was genuinely flirting. I didn't get it. She seemed to be attracted to him. Carter, for as long as I've known him, has been attracted to every female he's *ever* met, including lesbians. He's one of those guys who believe that some women are gay only because they don't want to be lonely while they're waiting for someone like him to come into their lives.

"Hey girl, you've done a nice job here." Simone put some hors d'oeuvres on her plate.

"Owen and Gary are the ones who've done a job. They cooked, brought the glassware, set up the tables, ordered the cut flowers, had the wine and liquor delivered and dusted and vacuumed every inch of the first floor. They insisted that they wanted to do a super job because of Kinshasa."

Simone smiled slyly. "I wonder why they would go out of their way to do such special things."

"Because they're special guys?" I teased back. I knew where Simone was going with this.

"That's true. Plus they've heard that Kinshasa is in the family." Simone leaned in close to me. "The word is out there, dear. You're the only one who's not convinced."

"I don't know about all that, Simone." I inclined my head toward the guest of honor and Carter. "Take a look over there."

We both watched as they seemed to be thoroughly amused with each other.

"I'd hate to think that I'm wrong." Simone paused, and then remembered her conversation with Charlene just a few moments earlier. Wanting to distract Corey from Carter and Kinshasa, she blurted out.

"Do you believe that Charlene brought a date?"

"That's our Charlene. Her name is Kate-something. She's a grad student." I answered Simone without taking my eyes off Kinshasa and Carter.

"A mere child. Charlene's reached her mid-life crisis. How does that old song go . . . "danger, heartbreak dead ahead . . ."?"

I nodded in agreement. "Charlene knows what she's doing. We'd better warn Kate, though." We grinned at each other.

"Corey, did you know that Carter was in town?"

"Nope. I was as unpleasantly surprised to see him as you were. He said he was here for the weekend; that he's going back to Martha's Vineyard in a day or two."

Simone stole a look at Carter and the writer. "The way he's getting along with Kinshasa, we might be seeing more of him this summer than we had expected."

That thought had crossed my mind, too. "And she seems to be getting along very well with him."

"She's got to be acting. He is so obnoxious, even straight women with common sense can't stand him after a minute. Why would a good looking single gay woman want to spend any time with him?"

"You won't give up, will you?" I looked at Simone straight in her eyes. "Kinshasa might not be gay, Simone."

"I tell you, she is."

I watched Carter bring Kinshasa another glass of wine. "I think you're wrong. But frankly, I wouldn't be surprised by anything that happened." I hoped that my facade of nonchalance wasn't transparent.

Kinshasa accepted the drink from Carter. But she excused herself after a moment and joined another group, attracted to it by the smoke stack of laughter rising above everyone's head. Carter watched her walk away and decided that she had the potential to make his periodic weekend trips home from the Vinyard worth his while.

"Wonderful party, Corey, wonderful! I knew that you could pull this together. Of all the instructors in our little summer group, I knew that you were the one who would do a splendid job!" Richardson George lavished his praise.

I smiled outwardly, but my heart wasn't in it. "Thank you. I imagine that Dean Phillips will want to host a reception during the fall semester, when the entire faculty is on campus."

Dr. George looked at me as if I had just told him that the wine he was drinking contained arsenic. "Uh . . . yes, yes. Good idea. Remind me in September, won't you?"

"I sure will." I eased away from my chairperson, not in the mood to tolerate any more of his inane chatter.

After a while, the guests began to leave. Some trekked through the house while others walked down the driveway toward the street. Charlene, Simone and Kate were huddled with Gary and Owen. I started to huddle with them, but decided to be the proper host and see how Kinshasa was faring. I looked around for our number one guest, but I didn't spot her at first. Then, in what was left of the twilight, I saw a quick jerking movement. Kinshasa wrenched her hand from Carter's. Half drunk, he was trying to pull her close to him. I walked toward them, clearing my throat as I got close.

"Kinshasa, I've been looking for you. Did you want to take the grand tour of my house now?"

Kinshasa looked at me with grateful eyes. "Yes. I'd like to do that." Turning toward Carter, she said, "I'll see you at the university in September, Dr. Washington."

Carter stood as straight as the alcohol in his bloodstream would permit, and hissed, "That all depends on how your house tour goes . . . Right, Corey?" His remark was not lost on Kinshasa.

"You've had too much to drink, Carter. Why don't you get someone to drive you home?"

I gently turned Kinshasa toward the house and gestured that she should enter through the back door. We left Carter in our wake, and went into the kitchen. Kinshasa leaned against one counter and I propped myself against the opposite one.

"You really don't have to take any tour. You're probably tired." I tried to sound sympathetic. "Being in the spotlight for hours isn't easy."

"You're right, especially when you have to fend off a very aggressive person. Thanks for understanding." Kinshasa flashed a quick smile and I had no difficulty understanding why Carter had been attracted to her instantly.

"I, . . . uh, thought that the two of you were getting along quite well, until I saw you pulling away from him."

Kinshasa looked directly at me, but avoided responding to my last comment. "What do you suppose he meant when he said his seeing me in September depended on how well the house tour went?"

I paused for what seemed like an hour. Well, here we go.

"It's a little complicated, Kinshasa." I began to speak, realizing that it was one of those rare times when I wasn't sure where my mouth would lead me.

"Carter can be very competitive with me, professionally and personally." Knowing that this explanation was as oblique as it was incomplete, I continued. "Carter and I have very different personalities, but we do share some things in common."

Kinshasa listened in silence. I had no choice but to go on. Exactly how I would go on, I wasn't sure. I just forged ahead, trusting my instincts.

"We like the same writers, and we'd both prefer to be writers who teach instead of teachers who write. We were tenured within a year of each other. He was first."

I couldn't think of any more fillers. I was going to have to be candid.

Inhaling deeply, I returned Kinshasa's direct gaze with my own. "And . . . it seems . . . that we're both attracted to women."

I paused for a second before going on. "If you're aware of my writing, then you must know that I'm a lesbian."

Although I spoke forthrightly, I felt that familiar edge of anxiety, and I was as ready to retreat defensively as I was to rejoice in receiving acceptance. My self disclosures had become easier through the years, but there was always that sense of taking a great leaping risk whenever I came out to someone.

"I guess that Carter thinks that my showing you the house is part of some grand seduction scheme on my part."

I stopped my monologue and waited for a reaction that didn't surface. "I assure you that it isn't."

Finally, Kinshasa broke her silence.

"I suspected that you might be gay. I know that your book was reviewed by the gay press, and my best friend's brother, who owns a book store, mentioned that you were on the Allerton staff." Kinshasa didn't lower her gaze. "For the record, your being gay is not an issue with me. So . . . if you're uncomfortable, there's no need to talk about it any further."

"*I'm* not uncomfortable at all." I stared into Kinshasa's eyes, looking for some evidence that would betray her claim of benign tolerance or let me know that it wasn't an issue for her because she, also, was gay. I saw no signs of either. Instead, she looked down at the floor boards for some way to end, or at least divert our conversation. I wanted to ease her discomfort.

"Why don't we leave Carter in suspense about the house tour? You and I will know that we were both too tired, but we won't tell him." I beamed at my solution, and felt relieved to see Kinshasa smile back at me.

"I don't really know Carter, having just met him this evening, but I'm inclined to say the hell with him."

"I've known him for a long time, and I'm inclined to agree with you."

Kinshasa winked her assent, and I tried to ignore where I felt the wink land. This woman had confused me. My reactions were way off balance. The last thing I wanted to do was allow myself to feel anything that I had to pay attention to.

"Corey, I can't thank you enough for doing all of this on such short notice. I know that you've been bogged down with your course and your students' work. This party was probably the last thing that you wanted to be saddled with."

I felt the atmosphere change. Kinshasa switched gears, becoming more formal, so I followed suit. "It was no problem. Your reputation is doing wonders for our department."

"That's very gracious of you. Do me a favor and tell the others that I thank them, also."

I walked with Kinshasa to the front of the house.

"Uh ... this is a little awkward, but I hope that what I told you about my personal life won't intrude upon our professional relationship."

I thought that I saw a trace of uncertainty flicker across Kinshasa's face.

"You haven't told me anything that I didn't already suspect. I respect you as a teacher and as a writer. And I envy your courage. Not everyone feels free and brave enough to be so honest ... I would imagine." She opened the door. "Good-night. And thanks again for the party."

Kinshasa turned and walked out to the porch, leaving her last words and the scent of her perfume draped all over me.

FOURTEEN

Images of the reception floated by Kinshasa lulling her to sleep. Warm green grass underfoot, the crisp taste of chilled wine, a rough insistent hand grasping hers, Corey's guarded confession . . . All of this swirled about her when the telephone suddenly rang.

"Hello."

"Kinshasa. Baby. It's me."

"Michael?"

"How are you? It's been awhile."

"How did you get this number?"

"When I'm determined, I get what I want."

"What is it that you want?"

"To see you, baby. It's been too long."

"It hasn't been long enough."

"Is someone there with you?"

"That's none of your business! I'm hanging up. I don't have anything to say to you."

"You're just not ready yet. But you will be and I can wait. We had too much going for us to just piss it away."

"We didn't have the right things going for us, Michael."

"That's not what I remember, Kinshasa."

"Don't call me again."

"I can't promise that, baby."

Kinshasa jammed the receiver into its cradle and unplugged the telephone. Many restless hours later she drifted into a fitful sleep. Memories of Michael, staler but stronger than those of the party, greeted her when Sunday morning arrived.

FIFTEEN

Simone and Karin stopped at my house one Saturday evening, and pulled me out to their car.

"Come on. We're tired of your sorry-ass excuses. You are going out with us tonight."

Karin drove and parked the car as close to MKDN's Place as possible. The entrance to the Luna Negra restaurant purposely eclipsed the club, its next door neighbor. The black and pink awning jutting out from the restaurant's facade all but hid the gray door that lead to the women's bar. Its discretely lettered name went unnoticed, I'm sure, by most of the restaurant's customers.

We walked in and looked around. Karin spotted a vacant table and steered us toward it. The cool, conditioned air covered our skin that a moment before had been hot and damp with July's steamy heat.

"What would you ladies like? The first round's on me." Since tonight was their idea, and Karin had driven, the least I could do was buy the drinks.

"I'll have a club soda." Simone was the self appointed designated driver.

"And I'll have a beer."

I walked over to the bar, a large rectangular island in the middle of the room. Almost every barstool was occupied. Some spots were two and three people deep. With one sweeping glance, I got the impression that most of the women were young. Some had a fresh, collegiate air. Others projected a hard-edged urban sophistication.

"What can I get for you, Corey?" Sonia Berceo flashed her brilliant smile.

It was then that I remembered that the Luna Negra and MKDN were owned by the same trio of women.

"Hi, Sonia. I'll take a Coor's Lite, a club soda and an Old Grand Dad with a twist."

"You must be thirsty." Sonia began filling the order. She set down the beer and the other two drinks.

"Here you are. That's nine even."

I handed her my money and started to ask if she was working until closing, but at the last second, I held onto my question. For some reason, I wasn't really in the mood to flirt.

A woman at the other end of the bar waved some money and diverted Sonia's attention.

"It's really crowded tonight. Typical summer Saturday. I'll catch up with you later."

I gathered some napkins, left most of the change on the bar and carefully made my way back to the table.

"When I saw who the bartender was, I figured that Karin and I would have a long wait for our drinks." Simone looked over at Sonia as she threw me her remark. "Did you leave her your last paycheck as a tip?"

"I left her an adequate amount, thank you. You know that I have undying respect for working women. Besides, Simone, she *is* cute."

"So I've noticed."

"Come on, Simone. Corey can afford to look." Karin stepped into the ring to defend me.

"Then why doesn't she ever look at Kinshasa Jordan?"

"You never miss an opportunity to go *there*, do you?"

Karin and I traded playful smirks. I appreciated her running interference for me. The more I get to know Karin, the more I value her qualities. I like the two of them as a couple. Simone is quick tongued. Karin is the processor, the thinker. She cares about people's feelings. It must be her compassion that helps make her a successful social worker.

Simone pointed at the door.

"Here comes our cradle robbing friend, Charlene."

As soon as Charlene's eyes adjusted to the dimness of the bar, she saw us, and walked to our table.

"Hey, everybody. Corey! As I live and breathe, is it really you? Here? At a bar? Having a drink and fun?"

"Yeah. I was thirsty." I smiled broadly.

"Very funny."

"What have you been up to, Charlene?"

"Oh . . . a little bit of this, and a little bit of that. Actually, I've had a busy summer so far, between teaching, working on a proposal and romancing."

Karin moved her chair so that Charlene could sit down.

"This is pure luck, running into you all, especially you two." Charlene gestured to Simone and me. "I need to talk to you about a project I'm organizing for the fall."

She leaned forward, locking us into her stare, defying us to pay attention to anyone or anything else.

"Before you get started, Charlene, would you like a drink?" Karin offered.

"No thanks, sweetie. I'm meeting Kate upstairs in a little while. I'll wait and have a drink with her."

Charlene seemed to dig her heels into the floor. "My project is a partnership between the university and an inner-city high school."

"You mean a black high school?" I had no time to play around with euphemisms. Inner-city always means black to me.

"Uh-huh."

"And you need two sistuhs, huh?" Simone had a huge grin on her face.

"You guys are double teaming me. I need some Allerton profs to work with the English teachers at the high school. Here's the deal. Our goal is to facilitate creative writing, especially short stories and poetry."

"Who's funding the project?" I asked this question pointedly, because my days of doing missionary work in the inner-city or in the suburbs were over.

"We have matching grants from the university and the Paul Foundation. I've already made two site visits to the school, and I've talked to the administrators."

Charlene paused, trying to gauge her friends' reactions to her plans.

"Interested, Corey?"

"I don't know. I haven't heard the details yet. What exactly would we do?"

"I need you to work with me once or twice a week, at the school. You'll have a group of seven or eight tenth graders who are interested in creative writing. We'll critique the kids' writing, and then work with each one individually." Charlene was practically breathless.

"And the final product?" Simone was curious.

"They'll develop a portfolio and the university will publish a collection of their work." She gave the table a "so there" thump.

I was practically hooked. "I think that I'm free on Thursdays. But you know, Charlene, I don't have any experience teaching high school age kids."

"I've already thought about that. Don't worry. Just think of them as students you'll be teaching three years from now in a freshman composition class."

"I'll think about it." I thought it was safer to leave a way out, in case it was the bourbon that was making the idea more attractive than it really was.

"Well, let me know soon. And what about you, Simone?"

Simone shook her head vigorously.

"No thank you, Ma'am. It's all I can do to handle freshmen. If I had my druthers, I'd be teaching only senior English majors."

Charlene smiled sympathetically at Simone. "I'm afarid that you'll have to wait for some of the old guard to retire."

Simone agreed. "I do happen to remember that Kinshasa Jordan is on a leave of absence from a high school position. And since she's also a writer, she might be a good person to tap for this project."

Simone nudged my foot under the table. I ignored her, but added, "She does have a point. Kinshasa knows how to work with teenagers."

"Sounds good. Thanks for the suggestion." Charlene winked at me. "If Ms. Jordan doesn't bolt the moment that I approach her, *and* if she agrees to participate, are you in Corey?"

"Yes." I made the commitment. "But I'll probably hate myself in the morning."

"Good! Now one more detail. You'll earn a small stipend, enough to cover meeting time and your gas into the city and back." Charlene leaned back in her chair. "Well, gang, time to party. Is anyone going upstairs to dance?"

I looked at Simone and Karin. Neither seemed inclined to move. "Not tonight. But you go on. Kate might be up there already."

"Okay. I'll see you both on campus on Monday."

Karin stood up. "Another round for everybody?" She went to the bar.

Simone cocked her head to one side and looked at me.

"If Kinshasa accepts, you owe me fifty per cent of your stipend."

"And why is that?"

"Call it a finders fee, honey."

"Give it up, Simone. Kinshasa is a colleague. I'll enjoy working with her because she's such a fine writer . . . and I know I'll learn a lot." I tried to sound convincing.

"You said you were going to learn a lot by attending her seminars, but you never went to single one. Why?"

"You are one relentless woman."

After missing all of Kinshasa's summer classes, I finally admitted to myself that spending *any* time in her presence, even in the safety of a sterile college classroom, was awakening feelings I wanted left buried. The last thing that I needed in my life right now was to feel even the smallest bit of desire for some woman who might or might *not* be gay.

"Yeah, I am relentless. So why didn't you sit in on one of her sessions?"

"I was too busy. And remember how interested she seemed to be in Carter Washington?"

Simone leveled her gaze at me. "You told me you thought that wasn't going any where, and that Kinshasa could see what a jerk he is. *I* made sure that she knows he's a *married* jerk with children. So what's standing in your way?"

"You're pushing me again, Simone."

"Sorry." She backed off. "I'm just trying to look out for you. I want you to be as happy as I am."

Karin returned with fresh drinks. By now, the over taxed ventilation system was not inhaling enough cigarette smoke. I covered my eyes with a damp napkin, welcoming the opportunity to break away from the uncomfortable conversation.

"Simone, is that Kinshasa sitting at the other end of the bar?" Karin pointed to a drinker's back.

"Where?" A rush of adrenaline snapped me to attention as I turned my chair around and strained to see through the smoky haze. The woman Karin had pointed to spun around on her barstool and revealed herself fully. She was not Kinshasa; only someone who, from a distance, bore a strong resemblance to her.

"Nope. It's not Kinshasa. False alarm." I hoped that Karin and Simone's preoccupation with each other would allow me to hide the disappointment that had settled between my shoulders.

SIXTEEN

Gayle Miller circled Kinshasa's block twice before she felt satisfied that she'd found the parking space closest to the apartment building. The Saturday morning drive from Long Island had been tedious. She stretched her legs, perched her sunglasses atop her head and picked up her overnight bag. Kinshasa lived on the fourth floor, so Gayle hoped that there was an elevator. She did not plan to break the kind of sweat that climbing four flights of stairs would require.

Kinshasa had been standing at her window looking for Gayle's car. So by the time that Gayle stepped into the lobby and began to scan the list of residents' names on the intercom board, Kinshasa was emerging from one of the elevators.

"Hello, Dr. Miller."

"'Shasa! Hi!" They hugged, genuinely happy to see each other. "You look great!"

"So do you, Gayle. So do you."

Gayle fingered the fronds of a palm planted near the elevator, and inspected the furniture and wall hangings while rocking from heel to toe on the thick carpet.

"Nice lobby. You can tell a lot about a building by its lobby. I'll bet your apartment is beautiful."

Kinshasa laughed at her friend's predictability.

"Somehow, I *knew* that you would say that."

There was nothing hidden or subtle about Gayle. Everything jetted to the surface. Kinshasa always felt comfortable because of her friend's open honesty.

The elevator door opened, and they walked to the end of the hallway where they made a right turn. Kinshasa's apartment was the third one after the turn.

"Oh, 'Shasa, it's big! And it looks like you've been here at least a year." Gayle took in the living room and nodded approvingly.

"I can really tell it's your place."

"Because you recognize the furniture?"

"Not just that. I see your things over there on the bookcase. And here are your favorite photos." Gayle picked up a portrait of Kinshasa's family.

"Where do you do your writing?"

"Well, I haven't done much writing yet, but I use the second bedroom as an office. All of my school things and my computer are in there. Go take a look if you want."

"I'm going to tour the whole place, so I hope you dusted."

"I knew you would, so I did. You don't miss a trick."

As Kinshasa guided Gayle from room to room, she remembered the tour of Corey's house that had never taken place. She still felt off balance, awkward about how that evening had ended. The awkwardness had increased by the time Kinshasa's writing seminar ended without Corey's having attended a single class. Kinshasa chided herself for sounding so flat and cold when Corey disclosed her sexuality to her. She figured that Corey had probably been put off by her reaction.

Gayle broke through Kinshasa's reverie.

"Shasa, you look relaxed and happy. This place must agree with you."

"I feel good, Gayle. Better than I have in a long time. I'm comfortable here."

"That's obvious." Gayle continued to take in the apartment. "So, tell me all about Allerton University."

Kinshasa paused before she spoke.

"The learning curve is steeper than I'd thought it would be, but I've learned a lot so far. The politics seem different here, and I haven't figured it all out yet. I enjoyed teaching the summer writing seminar.

It's so easy talking to older students." She laughed. "I might not *ever* want to go back to teaching in a high school."

"Why don't you resign?" Gayle had seen her friend undone many times by the stresses of her job.

"I'd have to think long and hard about that. I still feel a commitment to city kids."

"Maybe you could teach part time, or tutor in the city. Live off your royalties."

"My accountant has told me that my royalties won't keep a roof over my head."

"Guess I didn't realize that."

"I won't be totally out of touch with high school kids while I'm here, though. A professor in the English Department is organizing a collaborative program with a high school in Philadelphia."

Gayle leaned forward, curious.

"What will you be doing?"

"I'll be part of a small team of instructors working with the high school teachers and their students on a creative writing project. I don't know all the details yet, but I understand that the goal is to help the kids publish some sort of journal or magazine." Kinshasa sounded enthusiastic.

"If you've got the time and the energy, it sounds great. But what are the drawbacks?"

Kinshasa looked puzzled. "Drawbacks?"

"Who gets the major payday? Who gets rewarded for all the hard work?" Gayle continued, almost lecturing. "You and I both know that altruism is a myth. Somebody gets the money or the good press or the dissertation material. Who do you think it will be?"

Kinshasa measured Gayle's words. She respected her friend's experience-honed opinions.

"Well, the project is the brainchild of a Dr. Charlene Gray. She's already tenured, so she can't be doing this for her *own* advancement."

Kinshasa pictured Charlene, and thought about her first impressions of her. Now that she was beginning to know Charlene, those first impressions were melting away. She didn't really want to believe that Charlene would organize such an ambitious project simply to further her own career.

"Maybe she's bored, and needs a new challenge." She paused, and then added, "You know, Gayle, at first Charlene's personality reminded me of Michael's in some ways."

"And you want to work with her?" Gayle couldn't believe her ears.

"Doesn't make much sense, does it? One of the other instructors, Simone, convinced me that Charlene was on the up and up. But hey! This is too serious a discussion for such a beautiful Saturday afternoon." Kinshasa beamed at Gayle. "What would you like to do?"

"Why don't we go for a short ride. I'd love to see the town and the campus. If you do the driving, I'll treat you to a late lunch afterward."

"It's a deal." Gayle hugged Kinshasa spontaneously, and Kinshasa was astonished when she realized how long it had been since anyone had hugged her. And she though it ironic that, at the same time that she had company here in her apartment, she felt a cloud of loneliness pass over her. There was a mighty void, a hollow place in her world.

The two women filled the weekend with a constant flow of conversation and laughter. They caught each other up with what was going on in their lives.

Gayle gushed every detail of her love life . . . an older man, Stephen, a psychologist. She felt a strong attachment to him but she had no illusions about the relationship being the great love of her life. She was sure that her brother, Gerald, was her family's best example of marital material. He and his partner, Keith, had been together for eighteen years. The bookstore that they owned in New York was their joint venture. Gayle had always been proud of Gerald, and very comfortable talking about him with her best friend.

Kinshasa related as many incidents from her new life in Allerton as she could remember. Gayle's favorite anecdote, however, and the one that inspired the most curiosity, was that of the reception for Kinshasa at Corey's home. Gayle pressed Kinshasa for an accurate portrait of Corey Lomax. It seemed that, of all the people that Kinshasa described, it was Corey whom Gayle most wanted to bump into during the weekend visit. Kinshasa was almost annoyed by Gayle's rapid fire questions about Corey. And at one point, she went into her bedroom to retrieve her book, the collection of short fiction which bore Corey's photo on the rear cover.

Gayle turned the book over to examine the picture.

"So you bought her book?" Not giving Kinshasa a chance to answer, "She's attractive, "Shasa. Don't you think so? How old is she?"

"I don't know. I never asked her." Kinshasa didn't hide her sarcasm.

Gayle pressed on. "So what's her story?"

"I really don't know her story." Kinshasa had carefully omitted Corey's coming out to her the evening of the reception.

"Does she go away on the weekends?"

"Uh . . . I don't know *that* information either." Kinshasa watched Gayle put the book down on the coffee table, photo side up.

"Well, I'm sorry that we didn't run into her. I'd like to have met Corey Lomax."

"Why?"

"Because Gerald told me she's an excellent writer. It would have been nice seeing and talking to her."

Kinshasa gave Gayle a suspicious look. There was something that Gayle wasn't saying.

"And?"

"And nothing. But why don't you give her a call? She went to all that trouble giving you a party. And you mentioned that you felt you could trust her more easily than some of the other people in your department."

Kinshasa smiled guardedly. "Trust her? I believe that I said I liked her straitforward manner."

Getting closer to her prey, Gayle pressed on. "That sounds like trust to me. You could invite her out for a drink, or lunch. What could it hurt?"

"Gayle, you would make someone a wonderful Jewish mother." She put her hand on Gayle's shoulder.

"You need some friends here, Kinshasa. I can't come visit you every weekend."

"Thank you for small favors. You know, you're a pest when you worry about my social life."

"So what about calling her?"

"That won't be necessary, dear. Our project team is getting together tomorrow for a working lunch. I'll see Corey then."

"Oh, that's great. A working lunch. How social. What a perfect setting for getting to know someone." Gayle's smile lessened the effect of her sarcasm.

"Gayle." Kinshasa warned her friend with a mock serious tone.

"Okay, okay, I'll back off."

Gayle sighed and looked at her watch.

"I have to leave now anyway if I want to beat the Sunday traffic." She bent down to pick up her bag.

"Next time it's your turn to visit me."

"You bet."

They left the apartment and walked down the hall, arm in arm. Kinshasa pushed Gayle and her suitcase into the elevator.

"Good-bye. Drive safely and give me a ring when you get home."

The elevator's closing door took Gayle's good-bye from the fourth to the first floor. Kinshasa returned to her apartment, anxious to put the small details of her home back together.

She checked the bathroom to make sure that Gayle hadn't forgotten anything. Then she picked up the magazines and books that Gayle had given her. She saw that she needed to reshelve Corey's book, and as she picked it up, she automatically looked at the back cover. The photograph of Corey was a good one. It captured her broad smile and the dramatic waviness of her black-touched-by-silver hair. Her clear hazel eyes suggested an openness and strength of character that Kinshasa felt she could trust and admire.

Kinshasa figured that both she and Corey were about the same age, both kissing their mid-forties. She considered keeping the book on the coffee table, but then, in a quick change of mind, decided to return it to the night table beside her bed.

SEVENTEEN

Jennifer finished packing for the vacation in Nova Scotia. She was hanging her garment bag on the bedroom door when the phone rang.

"Hello."

"Jen? It's me." Pat sounded discouraged.

"Hi, honey. Everything okay?"

"Not really. We're understaffed down here. There's some kind of intestinal bug floating around." She paused, waiting for Jennifer's response. There was none. "So I won't be able to leave until my usual time, if then."

"You mean you can't leave before four?" Jennifer made no attempt to conceal her displeasure.

"Yeah. I'll get to the condo by four-thirty, pack and be at your place by six-thirty or six-forty-five. Don't hold dinner for me, just in case I get there later than that."

"Well, I hope you can sleep tonight. We're leaving for Portland real early."

"Don't worry, Babe. I'll go to bed as soon as I get there."

"Of all the detectives there, why do *you* have to pick up the slack? Why can't someone cover for you? It's the day before your vacation, for Christ's sake!"

"That's just the point, Jennifer. It's the day *before* I leave." Pat became defensive. "Look, if I can leave any earlier at all, I will. If I can't, then I simply can't. It's as easy as that."

"All right. I'll see you later."

"Bye."

Jennifer slammed the receiver down. She cursed the fact that Pat was so damned dedicated to her job. That job, with all of its ugliness, was bigger than both of them. It made Pat so tense, so difficult to talk to sometimes. Their relationship was no longer fun for Jennifer. It was hard work. And it seemed to Jennifer that she was the one doing most of the work. She picked up the phone again, and dialed a familiar number.

A recorded message told her that Corey was not in her office. Jennifer dialed Corey's home number, only to hear Corey's voice on another answering machine. Jennifer spoke into the phone.

"Corey, I've been thinking about you, and I wanted to hear your voice. Why don't we get together for lunch soon? I'll be out of town for the next ten days, but let's plan on seeing each other when I return. Take care and good-bye for now."

Jennifer wondered for a moment why she'd placed that call. Was she getting even with Pat? Was she that annoyed that Pat couldn't leave work early? Or were there still some unfinished feelings she had for Corey? Well, what was done, was done. Why should she question her motives?

EIGHTEEN

"Thank you, Dr. Washington." Kinshasa labored to be polite but formal as Carter opened the office door for her.

"Don't mention it. But please. Call me Carter." He stood back and all but shook his head in appreciation as he looked at Kinshasa's slacks clad thighs and hips. Carter knew how to disguise a frank leer with a facade of gentlemanly protocol.

"How do you like your office space?"

"Compared to what I'm used to as a public school teacher, this is luxurious. She still did not smile. She didn't want to repeat her earlier mistake and send Carter any signals that he might misinterpret.

"I was afraid that this space might seem small to you. Look over here at my office." He touched her elbow lightly and guided her from the open area of the office pod to his corner office.

"Just look at the view from that window."

Before she knew it, Kinshasa stood in front of the larger of two windows in Carter's office. Outside lay the campus green with its maple and oak trees shading the grassy oval. The office itself was organized neatly with framed diplomas, certificates and journal articles adorning one wall, and bookcases along another. There were a few photos of Carter in formal attire, Carter in tennis whites and Carter posed with small groups of students. Fraternity paraphernalia was strewn across one of the bookcase shelves.

"The view is beautiful, Carter." Kinshasa made a move toward the door, eager to return to the common area where there were more people.

"Come back to look at the view anytime, Kinshasa."

Carter moved aside, letting Kinshasa pass in front of him. He closed his door and looked at the empty space on top of his file cabinets, pleased with his cleverness at having removed the photos of his wife, Marie, and their two children, Chantelle and Carter, Jr. The Sunday after Corey Lomax's party, where he first met Kinshasa, he'd had the smarts to put the pictures inside a file drawer. He had plans for this writer, this Kinshasa Jordan. The same plans he'd had and had carried out with the best looking and most docile female students he'd taught during the past few years.

NINETEEN

It couldn't be the end of August already. I wasn't ready for the summer to end. But already I'd seen the formations of Canada geese flying over my backyard, and my electric bill was sky high from having the air-conditioner on night and day. So I knew it was time to deal with the reality of the rapidly approaching fall semester, and to start planning for Charlene's high school project.

A whole year had passed by since Jennifer moved out . . . a year and two weeks. Sooner or later she had to come over to get the few things she'd left behind. Maybe that's why she'd left a message on my answering machine a couple of weeks ago. What I didn't understand was that "I've been wanting to hear your voice" crap. She can forget that.

It's not as if I were dreading her visit. It seemed like a formality and nothing more. Mulling over the possible outcomes of my first foray into a high school took more emotional energy than thinking about Jennifer's coming by to pick up her things.

I poured myself a lemonade, added a shot of vodka and a splash of cranberry juice, and mulled over my memories of yesterday's meeting at Charlene's condo.

"So what are these people from Jefferson High like?"

"Very ordinary, but nice. You'll like Marsha Riley, especially."

"Why? Anything special I should know about her?"

"You'll figure it out as soon as you meet her." Charlene winked at me, and then went to answer the knock at her door.

Oliver Sullivan and Sarah Grossman walked in. Sarah's sprightly energetic pace traveled just slightly ahead of her voice.

"I'm so happy to meet you, Corey." Sarah thrust her hand toward mine, grabbed and shook it heartily.

"Hello." Oliver offered a reluctant, nervous handshake. "I'm Oliver Sullivan."

"Nice to meet you. I'm Corey Lomax."

I know that it's wrong to prejudge a person based upon the firmness of his handshake, so I hoped that Oliver wasn't as weak as his listless grip. He was a pleasant looking young man, neatly, if not stylishly dressed in a dull colored plaid shirt and khaki pants. His hair and mustache were both trimmed short. Because he appeared to be in his twenties and was African-American, I'd like to think that his students related to him. But something told me that he might fall short of connecting with them.

"Does anyone want a glass of iced tea?" Charlene took our beverage orders.

"I'll get it, Charlene."

I went into her kitchen and was filling the glasses when Kinshasa arrived. Oliver and Sarah must have been aware of her reputation. I could hear them fire questions and praise at her. She looked up at me as I carried the drinks into the livingroom.

"Hello, Corey." She had such a warm smile as she spoke to me. "It's nice to see you somewhere other than behind the desk in your office."

"Yeah, it's a miracle that I can still do things other than reading, writing and grading papers."

I self-consciously thought about my appearance and wondered if the jeans, tee-shirt and running shoes I had on were too casual for this meeting. Kinshasa must have read my mind.

"You look great . . . relaxed and less serious."

I followed the path that her eyes took and figured that she was reading the rainbow colored Provincetown graphic on my shirt.

"Green is a good color for you."

"Thanks." I prayed that the heat I felt spreading from my face to my ears hadn't turned me red. I didn't want to light up like a Christmas decoration.

Mercifully, there was a loud knock at the door. Charlene walked over, opened it and a woman who I figured must have been Marsha Riley strode into the room. She was, if possible, even more intense than Charlene. She hugged Oliver and Sarah, and, not waiting for any introductions, stepped toward Kinshasa and wrapped both of her hands around the writer's right one.

"Kinshasa Jordan, I recognize you from your books. We're absolutely thrilled that you're going to work with our kids!"

"Thank you. I'm looking forward to it. Believe it or not, I'm starting to miss the annual back to school rituals. So working at Jefferson High will fill that void."

"And we'll be the richer ones for it, I'm sure." Marsha looked my way, glided toward me and extended her hand. "And *you* must be Corey Lomax. I've read *your* books, also."

Oliver was bewildered. "You're a writer, too? What have *you* written?"

"Some short fiction." Somehow I guessed that a short answer would be enough for Oliver.

"*Excellent* short fiction!" Marsha punctuated my brief answer with her brilliant smile and a quick wink.

I guess I knew why Charlene thought that I'd like working with Marsha. She was, in a word, stunning. A full two inches taller than I, she had casually arranged reddish brown hair whose every wave screamed life. Her smiles seemed right on the surface. Deeply dimpled cheeks were a bonus. I'm cursed with this writer's imagination, so I speculated that Marsha had dimples in at least one other place, just waiting to be discovered.

Charlene gathered her flock in the living room. Methodically, she listed her objectives for the writing project, and listened to our feedback. Then, the six of us set up a schedule and paired off. I worked with Sarah and Kinshasa teamed with Oliver. It was Charlene's job to coordinate everything as Marsha jotted down notes and told us, from her vantage point as assistant principal, what was feasible and what was not.

Once in a while I looked toward Kinshasa and Oliver. She kept guiding him out of "I don't think we can do this" land. He didn't seem to be as impressed with Kinshasa's celebrity as he was with the enormity of the task ahead of them. More than once I heard Kinshasa say to him patiently, "Let's give it a try, Oliver. We'll never know if we assume that the students can't do this."

She was kind and gentle with him; kinder and gentler than I would have been.

Marsha was very generous with her smiles and an occasional pat on my arm as she stopped to listen to Sarah and me. I hoped to God that I could remember how to flirt back.

After three solid hours, we reached the point of diminishing returns and decided to pack it in for the day. Sarah left with Oliver in tow. Marsha dashed out in a blur, before I had a chance to test my flirting skills, but not before she had gotten Kinshasa and me to each fill out an index card with our addresses and phone numbers. I promised to call Charlene later and then I left with Kinshasa. The two of us walked toward our cars.

"Whoa! It is one hot afternoon, isn't it?"

The sun bounced angry heatwaves off the macadam in the parking lot. Just as I was about to suggest that we go out for a cool drink, I noticed Kinshasa massaging her forehead.

"Do you have a headache?"

She nooded and put on her sunglasses.

"I've had one all day. It's probably my sinuses acting up. The humidity does a number on them."

"Did you take anything for it?"

"A couple of aspirins a while ago. Right now, I just want to go home, take a shower and sit in front of the air conditioner."

I looked at her sympathetically, then blurted, "I was going to ask if you wanted to have a drink and maybe get an early dinner. But if you're not feeling well . . ."

Kinshasa shook her head.

"I'm really not feeling too great."

I paused, took a deep breath and hoped that my voice didn't reveal my sudden nervousness. " . . . this is probably not a good time to ask, but would you like to get together . . . sometime in the future . . . for dinner, or maybe a movie?"

"Thanks, Corey, but I don't think so."

There wasn't even a second's hesitation before her refusal.

I regrouped awkwardly.

"Okay. I hope I don't sound like I'm trying to make a date with you, because I don't want to embarrass or offend you. But I don't know if you've met many people here in Allerton."

I stared steadily at Kinshasa, trying to penetrate the darkness of her sunglasses, and to convince her *and* me of my sincerity.

"I'm not offended, Corey."

We stopped walking. Kinshasa stood perfectly arect and returned my direct gaze.

"And, actually I haven't met that many people here. But, unlike you, I don't open up right away and talk about my private life at the drop of a hat. I guess I think it's no one's business but my own."

I nodded slowly, weighing Kinshasa's admonitions. I felt duly chastised for coming out to her the night of the reception, and my ego smarted.

"You must be referring to my coming out to you after the party. And you seem to be uncomfortable. I'm sorry."

"I feel uncomfortable when people make assumptions."

"Do you think I've invited you to dinner and the movies because I'm making assumptions about your identity?"

This was clearly going someplace that I had not expected.

Kinshasa looked me dead in the eyes.

"I should think that you are too intelligent and sensitive a person to make assumptions about someone that you don't know."

This was one time when I didn't have a comeback. My initial reaction, to steer clear of Kinshasa, had been right. Simone could forget all of her fantasies about Kinshasa being a closeted lesbian. She was *beyond* closeted. She was turning down my offer of *friendship* for God's sake.

"Well, you're right. And you know what they say about that word "assume", Kinshasa. So I'll see you. Hope your headache gets better."

I had arrived at my car. Kinshasa gave a half-hearted wave and walked a little further to hers.

Unknowingly, Charlene had done me a huge favor. Marsha Riley looked good to me from the moment she arrived for the meeting. I hoped that Charlene's line that she expected I'd love working with her, plus Marsha's touchy-feely flirtation with me weren't leading me down the path of another false assumption, because Marsha was looking better and better to me as each minute passed by in that hot parking lot.

TWENTY

For the first time in months, Pat Adamson drove to work, to her new job, wrapped in a vague haze of sleepiness, but not depression and dread. Before parking and going into the building, she drove the perimeter streets around Jefferson High School, keeping alert for truants. Each day she varied the time that she did this. It didn't really matter what part of the school day she chose. There were usually some kids hanging around the nearby stores or the fast food restaurant.

Pat turned the corner and coasted in front of the school. Two girls, dawdling near the entrance, threw down their cigarettes and picked up their bookbags. They glared at Pat's slowing car and sauntered into the building. Then she accelerated, intending to turn one more corner to reach the staff parking lot. But the motion of flailing arms and fists caught her attention yards and yards before she reached the corner.

Instinctively, she steered the car to the curb, set the parking brake, shoved the gear shift into park, and jumped out to confront the trouble.

"Get the fuck into that building!"

"No! You can't make me!"

"The hell I can't! I'm your mother! You're going to mind me!"

A spare, wiry wisp of a woman was slapping a young boy with all her might. Veins pulsed in her face, from the upper edge of her cheekbones to the middle of her forehead. Her eyes shot sparks and her raspy smoke cured voice was strained to its limit. She grasped her son's arm with the force of a vise. The boy was small, not quite five feet tall. He was skinny, and wore his pants slung low, not because he was stylish, but because his waist was non-existent. His hair was long and uncombed. He tried to free his arm, twisting and wrenching it. But he lacked the strength that he needed to extricate himself from his mother's grip.

"Let me go!"

"You goin' into that school! And you goin' to learn. You hear me?" The woman didn't loosen her hold. She was dragging the boy with one hand, and reaching for the door handle with the other. The boy alternated between tugging away from her and swinging his fist, trying to land punches on his mother's chest and face.

"Stop! Hey!" Pat stood next to them and flashed her badge. "Stop!"

She looked at the boy and began to speak slowly and calmly.

"Your mother's going to let you go, and you're going to stop trying to hit her. Hear me?"

The boy stared back at Pat. He rested his fighting arm by his side and unfurled his fist. Pat turned to the woman.

"Let go of his arm, Ma'am."

The boy's mother slowly relaxed her grip and released her son's arm. Pat could see the faint bloody imprints that the woman's fingernails had left.

"You see what you done to my arm? Ahma call DHS." The boy massaged his wounds.

"I hope you *do* call DHS, 'cause I wanna go to Family Court with you, boy. Then we'll see who's not going to school."

The softness left Pat's voice.

"We're all going to go inside the building. Are you a student at Jefferson?" She glared at the boy.

"Yeah, he's a student here. And he keeps playin' hooky. He don't wanna go, Miss. But I'm here to tell you that he has to."

"Let's go to the office."

Pat opened the door and nodded to the non-teaching assistant who was there to greet visitors. She directed the mother and her son toward some vacant chairs outside of the office area.

"Let's all sit down here and talk for a minute." Pat looked over the office counter and locked eyes with one of the secretaries.

"Mrs. Stewart, could you call the Dean of Students and ask him to please come over here? Thanks."

She turned back to the boy. "What's your name?"

"His name is Raheem Ellis, and he's in the ninth grade." The mother took her son's voice away from him.

"Raheem, why aren't you attending school regularly?"

"I don't like it." Raheem answered Pat without looking at her.

"But it's only October. How do you know that you don't like it, so early in the semester?"

"He can't do the work. He never brings work home with him." Once again, the mother spoke for her son.

"I can so do the work. I just don't wanna." Raheem's eyes bore a hole into his mother.

"Then why don't you do nothin'? He's all the time tellin' me that the teachers, they don't give no homework. I don't believe that crap. Ain't that much changed since I went to school."

The mother sucked her teeth and looked disgustedly at her son. "You gonna fail! You know you gonna fail!"

"Calm down, Mrs. Ellis. Let's give Raheem a chance to speak." Pat turned to the ninth grader. "So what's the story? Do your teachers give you homework? Did they give you textbooks?"

Raheem stared ahead, sullenly. "Yeah."

Remembering snatches of a conversation between a counselor and a teacher that she'd overheard, Pat ventured another question, this time directly to the frustrated mother.

"Is Raheem a special education student?"

"I ain't in no special ed! I ain't dumb!" Raheem fired back.

"He used to be . . . in his old school. But here they put him in all regular classes. They say he ain't special no more. He's in the mainstream, or somethin' like that."

The mother punctuated her last sentence with a proud smile. She sat up straighter in her chair.

"It's like he learned so good, and accomplished so much at that old school. Now he's smart like all the regular kids. He got a regular roster, and he's gonna be bringin' home a report card with grades in regular classes." She beamed triumphantly.

Raheem recoiled from her praise. Huge tears rolled down his narrow cheeks, and he hung his head and muttered.

"I can't *do* the regular work. It's too hard for me. I be tryin', but the books . . . they don't make no sense to me. And when I ask the teacher for help, the other kids be callin' me "faggot and bitch ass"."

Mrs. Ellis touched her son's arm, trying to heal the welts left by her nails. *"Raheem,* why didn't you tell me all this?"

Raheem wiped his face. "'Cause you be mad at me all the time, and it ain't my fault."

"Detective Adamson?" Mrs. Stewart called Pat. "The Dean doesn't pick up. He's not in his office. Is there anyone else you'd like me to call?"

"Try the counselor, please. His last name is Ellis, and he's in the ninth grade."

Pat turned to Raheem and his mother.

"Ma'am, it's still early in the semester. Early enough, I would think, for Raheem to be able to succeed. When his counselor gets here, we'll explain the situation and get Raheem the courses he needs. Okay?"

"Yeah, that's fine." She lowered her voice and spoke to Pat. "I thought you was going to arrest us."

Pat smiled. "For a second, I did too. But we got the situation under control. And this is a talkable problem, right Raheem?"

"Yeah."

"Thank you, Officer." Mrs. Ellis smiled at Pat.

"That's okay." Every conflict around here should be so easy to resolve, Pat thought. But hey, this sure beats the crap she had to investigate when she was in the Special Victims Unit.

TWENTY-ONE

"**Y**ou need to get over it, Corey. Just because Kinshasa didn't want to go out for a drink and dinner doesn't mean that you can't show up to support her at her bookstore reading." Simone and Karin felt duty bound to go to this reading, and to drag me along with them.

"Gay or straight, she's a black woman living alone in a new place. We have to stand by her."

"Oh please." I rolled my eyes. "Next you'll start singing "That's What Friends Are For."

"We won't get *that* carried away. But we *do* need to support her."

The bookstore, Ex Libris, was brand new and very large. Merchandise was spread out on two levels. The obligatory espresso bar on the upper floor pumped out half a dozen different flavors of coffee, while the muted tones of a popular saxophonist's music wafted throughout the store.

I walked the short distance from my house and got there before Karin and Simone arrived. Although she couldn't see me from the table where she was seated, I saw Kinshasa, her profile alternately tipped upward, acknowledging a fan's comment, and downward, signing a copy of one of her novels.

"Glad that you came, Corey?" Simone shot me a knowing look.

"I haven't come in quite some time, thank you."

Karin laughed and Simone just looked at me pityingly.

"Well, who's fault is that?"

"That coffee smells good. Do you two want any?" Despite my smart ass answer, I was anxious to change the direction of our repartee.

"No thanks. We had dinner before we got here. But you go right ahead." Simone sat down on one of the chairs that I'd saved for us.

"That's okay. I'll wait. It looks like they're getting ready to start."

Simone looked over at me.

"Oh, before I forget, are you coming to Thanksgiving dinner at our house?"

I hit the side of my head with my hand. I had completely forgotten Simone's and Karin's invitation.

"I'd love to. Let me know what I can bring."

Simone gestured toward Kinshasa.

"Uh, I said *what*, not *who*."

"You can bring one of your famous sweet potato pies." Karin put in her request.

"And maybe you can pick up Kinshasa and drive her over. Give a woman a hand since she's new in town."

"She seems to be finding her way around town just fine, Simone. Have you invited her to the dinner yet?" I winked at my buddy, knowing how she procrastinated from time to time.

"No, not yet. But I'm going to. Maybe tonight after her reading."

"Well, good luck. Maybe you shouldn't tell her I'm going to be there. She seems to have an aversion to the idea of having dinner with me." I smiled as I said this, but part of me was serious.

We watched a young man escort Kinshasa upstairs to the area that had been set aside for her reading. By now, every chair was occupied. Kinshasa stepped up to the platform and rested her book on a lectern. She acknowledged the polite applause that greeted her, and began to read passages from her novel, the one about the black singer from Boston.

The audience was quiet, respectful, anxious to hear Kinshasa's poetic prose. Hers was a style that sounded as good to the ear as it looked to the eye. Her rich, controlled voice gave a new dimension to the characters. I listened as she breathed the protagonist to life, imbuing her with color and texture.

Suddenly, the magic exploded.

"You're a homophobe! You'll have the blood of gay men and women on your hands!"

I saw half a dozen people hurling a barrage of verbal assaults. One of the hecklers had been a student of mine, and I knew that she was a member of RESIST NOW!. She held a sign that read: "ZERO TOLERANCE FOR AN INTOLERANT WRITER!". A man kept chanting, "Ask Jordan about Raymond."

My mind raced. Who the hell was Raymond? Simone grabbed my arm.

"Corey! Raymond is the character we talked about. We thought Kinshasa might be homophobic because of him, remember?

"Oh damn! I forgot!"

Kinshasa stopped reading and stepped back from the lectern. She looked stricken. By now, the bookstore security people were forcibly pushing the demonstrators down to the lower level and out of the building.

"Do you think she'll be all right?" Karin wondered aloud and Simone shrugged her shoulders.

"I don't know. It's going to be hard for her to continue."

A few members of the audience applauded softly and encouraged her to go on with the reading. Kinshasa breathed deeply and adjusted her composure along with her eyeglasses. She resumed. But it was clear that she'd lost her honey-toned delivery. Her voice never regained its confident pitch. Little nuances got lost every time she felt the need to look around furtively, to protect herself from another surprise interruption.

When she finished, the audience applauded. Their hands sent a message of appreciation and relief. The manager made his way to the lectern and escorted Kinshasa from the riser to another room behind a closed door. It was clear that Kinshasa wouldn't be signing any more of her books tonight.

"Come on. We should see if she's okay." Karin made the first move, with Simone and me following her.

"She might need help getting home okay." Simone lobbied for us to be a three woman security force. "You know I support RESIST NOW!, but they've picked on the wrong person. Look over there!"

Simone pointed toward the bookstore's expansive front window. "They're still out in front, demonstrating."

Karin and I looked through the window. We could see the angry, chanting, sign carrying group of protesters. Most of Kinshasa's audience dispersed quickly. We reached the man who had guided Kinshasa away from the lectern. I had no reason to believe that he would do what I requested, but it was worth a try.

"Excuse me. Could you tell Ms. Jordan that when she's ready to leave, her friends from the university are here?"

He arched his brow, made a quick appraisal and lead us to a huge stockroom. A customarily cool and composed Kinshasa stood next to a pile of boxes, fear and concern stretched across her forehead.

"Simone thought that we should take you home. You know . . . like bodyguards." I winked at Kinshasa, trying to lighten the moment.

She smiled back wanly. "Sorry about the protestors."

"*You* shouldn't be sorry. Those fools outside are the sorry ones." Simone was a great cheerleader when she needed to be.

"Did you drive here, Kinshasa?" Karin took charge.

"Yes. My car is in the parking lot behind the bookstore."

"Let Corey get your car. She'll drive to the back door and pick you up. Simone and I will follow the two of you to your apartment building, then we can take Corey home."

"I really appreciate this." Kinshasa gave me her keys. I thought I could see her hand shaking.

My friends gave me a few minutes, then they left through the delivery entrance, got into the cars, and we drove, uneventfully, to Kinshasa's apartment. As I parked, Karin steered her car next to Kinshasa's and lowered her window.

"It doesn't look like anyone followed us. Do you feel pretty safe, Kinshasa?"

"Oh, sure. But why don't you all come in up for some coffee. I'm so grateful that you were there and were willing to help me."

Simone declined quickly. "Oh, thanks, Kinshasa. Maybe some other time. But Corey, why don't you stay? You never had a chance to get your coffee at the bookstore."

"And how will I get home?" Even as I asked, I knew that Simone had a solution figured out.

"I'll drive you." Kinshasa offered. "It's the least I can do to thank you for the escort service."

"That's a great idea! And Corey, tell Kinshasa about the Thanksgiving dinner invite, please?" Simone smiled sweetly at me and motioned to Karin to drive away. She had that smug, satisfied air about her, pleased that her impromptu scheme was playing out as planned.

I set the car's parking brake, removed the key from the ignition and gave it to Kinshasa. We walked into her building and she punched in her entry code. I couldn't help but wonder if Kinshasa remembered my dinner invitation and her refusal in Charlene's apartment parking lot. And if she did, how was she feeling right now as I was about to enter her home?

"I'm on the fourth floor."

I nodded. "I'm glad the RESIST NOW! folks don't know where you live."

"So am I."

A moment later, we were in her apartment.

"Why don't you have a seat while I fix some coffee?"

"Thanks." Instead of sitting down right away, I read the titles of the books I saw in her bookcase and looked at the photos on the shelves.

"Are the people in the large photo your parents?"

Kinshasa looked out from the kitchen. "Yes they are."

"You look like a younger version of your mother. She's very attractive."

"Thank you. I needed that compliment."

Then she added, "My mother died a few years ago, and I still miss her terribly. My father just retired, and he seems to be doing well. Between golf and fishing, he stays very busy."

Kinshasa's mood brightened. She offered me one of her rare smiles and I wondered if we couldn't be friends after all. Despite what she might think, I do know how to be a friend to a woman. I don't consider every attractive single female to be a potential lover.

"Is it all right if I join you in the kitchen?"

"Sure, come on out."

I resisted the temptation to answer that I'd come out a long time ago. No sense in queering the deal now.

Kinshasa reached up to a cabinet. "Do you take sugar and milk in your coffee?"

"Nope. Just black." I accepted a mug of steaming coffee. Looking over the top of it, I braved a question. "Has anything like that ever happened to you before at a public reading?"

"No. This was the first, and I hope last time. My writing has been criticized of course. I'm used to that. But this was more like a personal attack."

She looked up at the ceiling, searching for a memory.

"A gay magazine once accused me of being homophobic because of that character, but I've never been the target of a demonstration."

I stared at the dark liquid in my mug.

"This might be poor timing on my part, Kinshasa, but I need to ask you something. Do you think that you *might* be homophobic? I'm thinking about that character, and . . . you were real quick to say that you wanted no part of going out to dinner with me."

Kinshasa didn't even blink.

"Well, first of all, I created Raymond's character with the belief that there are gay villains as well as gay heroes . . ."

"I can't disagree. I know that's realistic. But gay people are very sensitive right now about how we're portrayed in books, on TV, in movies. If I remember correctly, Raymond is not only psychotic, he dies of AIDS, doesn't he?"

"He does." Kinshasa's curt reply warned me to tread lightly.

"Well, I don't have the gall to sit here in *your* kitchen, drink *your* coffee and sermonize, but can *you* understand why RESIST NOW! would demonstrate?

"Of course I understand." Kinshasa paused and chose her next words carefully.

"Corey, I need you to understand and believe that I am not homophobic. I've written about all kinds of African-American men and women . . . heroes and villains. Some of them are righteous, and others are downright evil. That doesn't make me *blackphobic*."

We both grinned at her manufactured word.

"Besides," she continued, "if I were homophobic, would I befriend you and Simone and Karin? And what was Simone saying about a Thanksgiving invitation?"

"Yeah. Thanks for reminding me." Maybe it was good to bring up the holiday invitation now. Because what I *really* wanted to ask about was Kinshasa's "befriending" me. Is *that* what she called it?

"Simone and Karin are having a few people over for Thanksgiving dinner, and they wondered if you'd like to join them?"

I looked at Kinshasa for some sign of indecision to flicker in her eyes, but none was there.

"I'd love to."

I was amazed at how quickly Kinshasa accepted the invitation. Apparently, she felt okay about being in *their* lesbian presences, just not in mine.

"Can I bring something? A salad or a dessert?"

"You'd better ask them about that. I've already signed up to bring a sweet potato pie."

"Is that one of your specialties?"

"Yes it is."

That and a few other things which you'll never get to taste. I smiled sweetly hoping not to betray my real thoughts.

"Do you have any Thanksgiving specialties?"

My question went unanswered. It got tangled in the ringing of the telephone.

"Hello? No. I have company, so it's not a good time to talk."

Kinshasa turned her back to me.

"A friend. That's none of your business, Michael." Her tone hardened and broke into brittle syllables.

"We've already settled that. Please don't call here again."

Kinshasa's shoulders caved in under the weight what appeared to be her second verbal assault of the day. She turned around and faced me.

"Is there anything wrong, Kinshasa?"

"Not any more. There used to be." She carried the empty mugs to the sink. "That was my ex, Michael."

"This hasn't been a very good day for you . . . I'm sorry."

"Don't be. It's history." Kinshasa leaned against the counter.

"I remember your telling me that you don't hang up your dirty laundry in public, so I probably shouldn't be asking you this question."

Kinshasa's calm stare didn't censor me.

"But . . . is Michael the reason you took a leave of absence and accepted the position at Allerton?"

The second I finished my question, I saw Kinshasa's eyes shut me out.

"Michael is the reason I decided to change my direction. But I don't believe in dwelling on sob stories. So the short version of my tale is that it was an abusive relationship, mentally and physically. After a while I got healthy and broke away. End of saga." Kinshasa waited for me to say something, but I kept my silence.

"Would you like another cup of coffee?"

"No thanks." I was suddenly very tired, having learned more about Kinshasa than I had planned.

"I need to get going. I could take a cab, you know. You don't have to drive me home."

"Not on your life. You, Simone and Karin were real friends to me tonight. Please let me return the favor."

There was a lot left unsaid between us as we rode toward my house. The very volume of it hung silently over our heads. Kinshasa kept the car's engine running as I got out. Now it was my turn to thank her. I did so, solemnly, locking the car door and my long denied attraction to Kinshasa behind me.

TWENTY-TWO

The cornerstone at Jefferson High School read 1982. But, like the students it served, the building was growing old before its time; forced to witness life, injury and death before reaching its twenty-fifth birthday.

Kinshasa, Charlene and I marched in during the first week of October. Kinshasa had a fair idea of what awaited us. I was full of ideas that I wanted to try with my students, but devoid of any notion of the realities of a large city high school. I figured that it would not be the same as *my* high school experience, but I didn't have the first clue about how very different it would be. So, totally unaware of my new environment, I steamrolled into Sarah Grossman's sophomore English class.

The graffiti punctuated entrance to Sarah's classroom was but a prologue to what I found on the inside. Five foot long literary quotations, pictures of famous writers and inspiration themed posters were plastered over most of the walls. Some thirty odd students slouched, sprawled or spilled out of desks that were loosely arranged in a circle.

"Class, this is Ms. Lomax, the writing professor from Allerton University. She's going to work with us this year on a writing project."

Acknowledging Sarah's introduction was the last coherent thing I remember doing that entire period. Competing with all the restless loud voices became a losing battle. I considered my efforts a failure, until the bell rang, and one girl, struggling against the tide of departing bodies, reached me.

"Hey, Allerton! You gonna teach us to write?"

I beamed at her, gamely. "I'm going to try."

"Good, 'cause I still have trouble makin' some of the capital letters in cursive. Ever since the third grade I been havin' trouble wif that."

Words failed me, for once in my life.

I lamely told Sarah that I wanted to see more of the school, (and of course, Marsha Riley's office), so she suggested that I start my tour before the next bell rang.

"The hallways get pretty crowded. We wouldn't want you to get lost."

I was headed toward the door, wondering if Sarah's "pretty crowded" was code for something else, when I heard a huge, dangerous, rolling thunderclap of approaching adolescent voices. As the tornado got closer, I remained galvanized, unable to retreat, incapable of going any further into the hallway. Sarah walked quickly to me and propelled me back into the classroom. Then, she went to the doorway, looked into the hall, ripped open the door of a wall mounted phone and punched out a phone number.

The air was filled with screams and expletive combinations I hadn't ever imagined. I could touch the anger and see the fear wafting in the hallway outside of Sarah's classroom. Loud bells chiming a code mixed with the electronic crackle of walkie-talkie distorted voices. Two blue uniforms flew past the doorway.

"Corey, why don't you sit down at my desk? Things are going to be in a shambles for a little while." Sarah offered me her chair.

"What's going on?"

"Just a fight between two girls. Probably another one of those he-said-she-said deals."

Sarah looked at me apologetically. "Sorry you had to be here now, but that's all a part of high school, you know."

"At least I wasn't in the hallway when it started. I wouldn't have known what to do."

"You bet."

Sarah went back to her classroom door, looked into the hallway for minute, then walked back toward me.

"Charlene and Kinshasa are probably waiting for you by now."

I looked in the direction of the hallway, not sure that I was ready to brave the trip back to the first floor.

"You'll be okay. It's quiet out there now." Sarah touched my arm and smiled kindly.

"You're not going to be scared off, are you? Our kids really do need this writing program."

"Don't worry, Sarah. I'll be back next week. I'm anxious to get started. I promise."

I could talk a good game when I had to.

I went out to the hallway, halfway expecting to see signs of combat. As I stepped over the area where the fight had been, I spotted tufts of hair and splotches of still damp blood dotting the worn carpet. By the time I reached Kinshasa, one floor below, I could hardly conceal the alarm I felt.

"Was it like this in the school where you taught?"

"Once in a while." Kinshasa examined my face, trying to decide how much she should say about the school in New Haven where she'd taught for so many years.

"But, you can't dwell on the negatives, Corey. You learn very quickly to look for the small victories and celebrate them."

I shot her a look of pure skepticism. Two hours after zealously entering Jefferson High, I walked numbly toward the exit. My spirit was like putty, and I realized that I would need remolding in order to fit into this situation.

TWENTY-THREE

Marsha Riley thumbed through a short stack of three by five cards, and found Corey's home phone number. She thought that she'd been so clever when she'd suggested that the Allerton instructors write their office *and* their home numbers for her personnel information file. She wasn't at all interested in Kinshasa's phone number. She was cute, but she wasn't Marsha's type. It was Corey she felt drawn to. There was something about Corey's eyes that radiated mischief. Something about her mouth that suggested sensuous pleasure. And the fact that she was an out lesbian made her all the more attractive. She dialed Corey's number, but no one answered. So she studied the card again, and then called Corey at her office.

"English Department. Corey Lomax speaking."

"Corey? Hello, it's Marsha. I'm so sorry that I missed you yesterday."

Juggling several emergencies at once, Marsha hadn't had time to take Corey around the school, or even to meet with her in her office.

"Oh, that's okay, Marsha. I figured you didn't have any time to spare. The pace seems pretty hectic there."

"You're right about that, Corey. Listen, I know that there was a fight while you were here. Sarah told me you were quite upset. I hope that it won't influence your plans to work with our students."

Marsha pictured Corey sitting at her desk, smiling into her telephone. She felt an all too familiar sensation of warmth spreading from her flushed cheeks and rushing through her chest, belly and down to her toes as she imagined herself sitting across from the Allerton professor. Marsha's preference for women of color was not a secret from anyone who knew her.

"No. I'm not discouraged. Sarah told me that fights are one of the facts of life in a city high school these days."

"Well, most days are better than yesterday was."

Marsha crossed her fingers around that lie.

"So, I'll look for you next Thursday?"

"That sounds great, Marsha. I'll expect to see you then."

Marsha put down the phone and crossed her legs tightly. She allowed herself the luxury of a daydream about Corey, in which she fantasized about running her fingers through the densely waved hair atop Corey's head . . . and elsewhere. A hard knock at her office door broke into Marsha's fantasy.

"Come in!"

In stepped the newly hired police detective, Pat Adamson. Marsha knew that adding another officer to the anti-violence initiative could only make her job a little easier, so she welcomed Detective Adamson.

Pat strode over to Marsha.

"I got a message over an hour ago that you wanted to see me, but I was hung up talking to those two girls who were involved in the big fight yesterday. They told me that the whole mess started outside of school, in the neighborhood. I was trying to get a handle on it before it escalated any further."

"Good. Don't worry about not coming *here* right away."

Marsha knew immediately that she was talking to a valuable ally. She figured that Pat was probably gay, to boot. This was a bonus.

"I wanted to touch base with you about another student, Tashna Barnett. She's a senior, nineteen years old. Her boyfriend beat her up pretty badly a couple of nights ago. I hope it's not too late to do something about it."

"I'll talk to her. Sort of an informal interview. I'll look for bruises or other injuries. Then I'll call it in to the domestic abuse unit, if you'd like. Somebody will be here before the day's over."

"Thanks." Marsha appraised Pat. "You're very efficient, detective. I'm glad that you're working with us. God knows we need all the help that we can get."

Pat smiled a "You're welcome", and then turned around and walked toward the door.

TWENTY-FOUR

J waited for the last of Simone's students to be out of earshot before I peeked into the classroom.

"Here's some news that will sharpen your little cupid's arrow."

"Hey, what's up, Corey?" Simone motioned for me to come closer.

"Remember I told you about Marsha Riley, the Assistant Principal at Jefferson High?"

I didn't give Simone a chance to answer. "She just called me. Said she was *so sorry* that she missed seeing me at Jefferson yesterday."

Simone smiled broadly. "So you think that Marsha's going to give you some play?"

"I didn't say all of that, Simone."

"So where are you going with all this?"

"Back to my office to do some work before the staff meeting."

"Smart ass." Simone's chuckle trailed off as I walked down the hallway. I was headed back to the building next door when I heard Kinshasa's voice.

"Corey! Wait! Going back to the department office?"

"Yes, you too?"

Kinshasa fell in step with me, covering the distance between the two buildings very quickly. We talked to each other pretty casually these days, more comfortably than we had a few months before. I was about to make a snide comment about our upcoming staff meeting, when I noticed two familiar figures in the distance.

"Do you know what time the meeting begins?"

I looked at my watch as we kept walking. "In half an hour."

The two figures were closer to us now. They stood near each other, facing the elevator. The door must have opened, because the taller of the two gave the other one a quick, furtive hug, and then disappeared into the open space of the lift. The shorter woman continued standing there, watching us, until we arrived.

"Hi, Corey. How are you?"

"I'm fine, Jen." I turned toward Kinshasa. "Have you two met each other?"

"No. Not yet." Jennifer stepped forward and stuck out her hand. "Hi. I'm Jennifer Renfrew. I suspect that you're the reason for our increase in admissions applications."

"Oh, I don't about that."

"We've been busier than we usually are this time of year. A lot of early decision candidates."

"Is that good or bad?"

"It's very good for the university, and especially for your department."

Jennifer could be charming when she wanted to be.

"Corey, did you get my last phone message?"

"Yeah, I did, Jennifer. Sorry I haven't gotten back to you."

I sensed Kinshasa moving away a bit, deferring the rest of the encounter with Jennifer to me and preparing to excuse herself. I wanted her to stick around, and wished that I had telepathic powers and could will her to stay.

"That's all right. I know you're busy. I called because I never finished collecting everything I . . . uh . . . left." Jennifer tried to be tactful in front of Kinshasa.

"Come over whenever you'd like. And feel free to bring Pat. Wasn't she here just a minute ago?"

"Yes. We had an early lunch and she had to get back to the city."

"Come over any time, Jen. Just give me a call first."

I was genuine with my invitation. I'd been wanting to divest my home of Jen's belongings for months now. And at long last, I was totally at peace about Pat Adamson. I even suspected that I might like her if I gave her a chance. Being a cop and having a relationship with Jennifer might not be the easiest things to do simultaneously.

"Thanks Corey. It'll be very soon."

Jennifer acknowledged Kinshasa. "It was a pleasure meeting you, Ms. Jordan. I hope that you enjoy all of your experiences here this year."

Was it my imagination, or did Jennifer tilt her head in my direction and suppress a smirk when said "all of your experiences"?

"I'm sure that I shall." Kinshasa smiled graciously.

"I'll give you a call, Corey." Jen gave me one of her long, soulful looks.

Kinshasa and I continued the trek to our offices. The little bit of tension that I'd felt while talking to Jennifer dissipated. Kinshasa matched my stride. She was quiet. I saw her looking at my profile. She might have been curious about my interaction with Jen. But she's so much into privacy, I knew that she wouldn't ask. So I offered an explanation.

"That was my ex." I had no trouble getting that out, albeit dispassionately.

"It must be difficult running into her at work."

"Not really. Enough time has passed, so it's not nearly as difficult now as it used to be." I just smiled and hoped that Kinshasa understood.

She jabbed me in my arm. "Well, Dr. Lomax, excuse me for saying this, but if you continue to flirt with Marsha Riley at our little group meetings, running into *her* at Jefferson might become difficult."

I cocked my head and looked directly at Kinshasa. "Do you think that I flirt with Marsha? Am I that obvious?"

"Most assuredly."

"And I thought that I was subtle."

"Not at all."

Although she was smiling and teasing me as she said this, I thought I detected the slightest trace of reproach in Kinshasa's eyes. I watched her retreating figure go into her office, picked up my mail and sat down at my desk. Instead of listening to my recorded phone messages, I stared straight ahead and wished that my flirting with Marsha *would* bother Kinshasa, if only just a little bit. Then, I remembered our encounter in the parking lot, Kinshasa's absolute lack of interest in going out with me, and a man named Michael who had been an important part of Kinshasa's life. A better use of my time, I was concluding, would be to think a little bit more about Marsha Riley.

TWENTY-FIVE

Carter Washington knew that Kinshasa was in her office. He had watched her talking with Corey in the hallway, and then disappear behind her closed door. They had a good ten minutes before they had to be in the staff meeting. He realigned his tie and entered her office quietly.

Kinshasa, busily examining some material in her file cabinet, had her back to the door as Carter approached stealthily. The carpet silenced his footsteps, and Kinshasa was too absorbed in her work to sense his presence. He placed his hands around her waist.

"How's it going, Kinshasa?"

Kinshasa spun around. In a second she forcibly removed his hands and pushed him away from her.

"Carter, don't ever do that again! I never gave you permission to touch me!"

Carter raised both of his hands in mock defense.

"I'm sorry. I didn't realize how sensitive you were." Carter suppressed a fleeting memory of Kinshasa going into the house with Corey, the night of the party, the night too much wine had loosened his inhibitions and convinced him prematurely that Kinshasa was ripe for the picking. "I was only trying to be friendly."

"That was *more* than being friendly. That was pretty close to harassment!" Kinshasa glared at Carter.

He stood his ground, remembering how she had laughed at his jokes, touched his arm repeatedly and allowed him to touch her in return.

"You didn't seem concerned about harassment a couple of months ago, when I touched you several times at Corey Lomax's party."

Kinshasa flashed back to that night, to the negative and suspicious feelings about Charlene that had conjured up memories of Michael and had lead her, stupidly, to flirt with Carter. If she hadn't been so intent upon erasing every vestige of Michael from her life, she wouldn't have felt such a vehement distrust of Charlene, who, at that time, seemed to be Michael's double. She cursed herself for having encouraged Carter's attentions. Now, seeing his mocking eyes and patronizing posture, she asked, "What do you want, Carter?"

"Simply to say hello and to see how the semester has started for you."

He took advantage of her diminishing anger and sat down in the chair next to her desk. Kinshasa remained standing.

"The first time I saw you at Corey's, I got the vibe that we might enjoy each other's company. Then, I seem to remember that she was going to show you her house, literally and figuratively. Did she?"

Kinshasa recalled her secret pact with Corey, but she decided to be forthcoming.

"No. I didn't get to see her house. We were both pretty tired that evening."

Carter leaned back in the chair and took in every part of Kinshasa. Buoyed by his assumption that Kinshasa and Corey had become neither close friends nor lovers, he cleared his voice and leered.

"What's your schedule like? We could go out for a drink sometime soon."

Kinshasa felt pure anathema for him.

"I'm very busy, Carter. I don't have much free time." She thought that any free time *he* had needed to be spent with the wife and children he never mentioned.

Not the least bit discouraged, Carter continued.

"I heard that you're working with Charlene Gray's project in that city high school. I heard, also, that you caused quite a commotion at your bookstore reading."

"You've heard quite a lot, haven't you?" Kinshasa knew that she was obliged to go one on one with him. "I survived the 'commotion', to use your word."

"What was it now? That RESIST NOW! group? Those faggots and dykes are outrageous. They staged a demonstration on campus last winter. Something about the university's health service bending to the board of trustees by not making free condoms and HIV testing available. Then they wanted to ban the military from recruiting here! What a mess! Damn faggots and dykes!"

Carter's face was distorted with self-righteous anger.

Kinshasa planted her feet firmly in front of him.

"Despite the fact that they accused me of homophobia, you need to know that I do support gay rights issues. RESIST NOW! had every right to protest that night."

She paused to make sure he was listening.

"And I have trouble hearing you use those terms to describe a minority group. I would have thought that someone with your education and worldly experiences would be more tolerant, Carter."

Kinshasa wondered if the university had a gay-straight student support group. Carter supplied every reason she could think of for one to exist. She made a quick mental note to ask Corey or Simone.

Carter's lips spread an insinuation.

"Well, it looks as if we could add a few more words under your name on your office door. 'Ms. Kinshasa Jordan, standard bearer for the sexually harassed and the gender confused'".

Kinshasa strode toward the door.

"Dr. Washington, you are as ignorant and as insensitive as you are arrogant." She gestured for him to leave her office.

As he walked by, he leaned into her and hissed, "Know what I think? I think you should spend more time with Charlene Gray and Corey Lomax. In fact, why don't you go across the hallway to Corey's office right now? Tell her that you want to take that tour of her house."

Kinshasa refused to respond to the bait. She waited until he was yards away from her door before she closed it.

On her way to her desk, she moved the chair that he'd been sitting in. She didn't want it near her. Kinshasa sat down and examined her appointment calendar. Counting backwards, she calculated how many months it had been since she left Michael, salvaged her self esteem and had last been held in loving arms. The total number of days and nights that had passed astounded her.

TWENTY-SIX

I popped the two sweet potato pies in the oven, set the timer and sat down with the morning newspaper and the tv's remote control in front of me. I'm not a fan of daytime television, so absentmindedly, I switched channels, alternating between the Macy's Thanksgiving Day parade and Philadelphia's. Naturally, I felt an allegiance to the Philly spectacle because it was more local than the other one. As luck would have it, I tuned in just in time to see a collegiate marching band from one of the historically Black schools. No one but no one could march in a parade quite like a Black college band. I smiled and yelled at the tv as the drumline filled the screen.

Soon after that, the odor of cinnamon and nutmeg reminded me that I hadn't decided what time I was going to leave for Simone and Karin's, not to mention what I was going to wear. There was no need to pick out anything spectacular. It was a safe bet that there would just be the six of us: Karin, Simone, Kinshasa, Charlene, Diana, (Charlene's current cutie on duty) and me. No need to dress to impress Kinshasa. I was past entertaining any thoughts in that direction. She's unattached, but she's definitely not family. So I don't need to get stressed out about my wardrobe. Obviously, she isn't homophobic, since she's having a holiday dinner with five lesbians. Maybe she's doing research for her next novel.

A few hours later, we all sort of arrived at Karin and Simone's front door at the same time. Everybody, that is, except Diane, who had decided at the last minute to fly home to Chicago to see her family.

Simone and Karin lived in a single story house, an anomaly in Allerton where most of the houses had two levels, and some of the older ones had three. Their block had several ranch style homes plunked down among the American and Dutch colonials. It looked like a disciple of Frank Lloyd Wright had been given five or so empty lots, and been told to fill them with Wright-style houses. From the outside, Simone's and Karin's house was an expanse of fieldstone, wood and glass.

"Come on in, everybody! Welcome!"

Simone took our jackets and hung them in the coat closet near the entrance, while Karin helped us unload the goodies we'd all brought.

"I thought that you'd like some wine, but I couldn't decide what kind. So I brought four bottles, two reds and two whites." Charlene had to laugh at her own expansiveness.

Simone took two of the bottles out of Charlene's hands.

"This is a dinner party, girl, not a wine festival. And there's only five of us now that your sweetie decided to go home for the break."

"I know that. But since Diane can't be here, I'm drinking for two."

"Then you might as well turn in your car keys now, because we're not going to let *you* drive home." I grinned at Charlene as I walked toward the kitchen with the pies.

"Kinshasa, the flowers are wonderful."

Karin took the blooms from Kinshasa and held them a little away from herself to admire their beauty.

"I'll go get a vase and water for them."

I agreed that indeed the flowers were lovely. And so was Kinshasa. She was wearing brown tweed light wool slacks and a softly hued gray knit top that emphasized her carmel skin and deep brown eyes. But why was I noticing and where was I going with all of this?

"Did you get them at that new floral store on Central Avenue?"

"Yes I did. I'm glad that you like them."

"Let's go into the great room. We already lit the fireplace."

Simone lead us into the largest room of their house. I gravatated toward the full wall fireplace. The stone surround and hearth were made of the same gray, tan and yellow-beige fieldstone that faced the house's exterior. I could feel the warmth radiating from the firebox, as I sat down on a floor pillow. Much to my surprise, Kinshasa sat on the other pillow, facing me. Simone poured us each a glass of wine.

"Simone, your home is beautiful. This room is so big."

"Thanks Kinshasa. Do you like modern architecture? Or are you more like Corey and Charlene who prefer older styles?"

"I admire some elements of both, I suppose. I don't like the minimalist look with a lot of glass and metal."

Charlene sat down on the sofa and contributed her two cents.

"Me neither. It's cold and sterile, isn't it?"

"It doesn't have to be. If you use bright bold colors you can heat it up. Right Simone?" I liked what she and Karin had done in furnishing their house.

"The fireplace adds a lot of warmth to the room. I'm so glad that I have one in my apartment." Kinshasa gave me a tentative smile.

"You're lucky. It's not always easy to find an apartment with a fireplace." I looked over at Charlene who was making her pitch to watch a football game on the tv in the adjacent den.

"Aw, come on, Simone. We're lesbians. We love football."

"Speak for yourself, Charlene. *I* do not love football. And we're not *all* lesbians. Excuse her please, Kinshasa."

Kinshasa had an amused look on her face.

"No problem."

"We'll keep the volume down so we can still hear the conversation in here." Charlene was almost begging.

"If you turn that tv on, there won't *be* any more conversation in here. Karin and Corey will desert us. I don't know about Kinshasa. Kinshasa? Are you into football, too?" Simone knew that it was a losing battle, but she was willing to skirmish.

Kinshasa quickly took a side.

"Not when there's the potential for so much good talk."

"Wrong answer, Kinshasa." Charlene tried to muster her troops. "Corey, you up for watching the game?"

"Usually I am. But Simone has gone to so much trouble today."

I pointed to the large square glass cocktail table.

"Look. She's put out hors d'ouevres for us. There's a soothing jazz cd playing. We can smell the turkey roasting. There's a great fire burning here in the fireplace. I don't have the heart to leave this room. The sister has worked too hard to give us all this." And okay. I still enjoyed learning more about Kinshasa. I wouldn't be able to do that if we were in two different rooms.

"Thank you, Corey. At least *someone* appreciates all the preparation that I've done." With that, Simone playfully glared at Karin who turned and looked sadly at Charlene.

"Sorry, Charlene. But if I want to continue living here, I'll have to settle for seeing the game highlights on tonight's sport's news."

"Coward."

Karin parried with Charlene. "I hope you're not taking it out on me that Diane decided to go to Chicago, are you?"

"Not at all. When you're involved with a beautiful younger woman, you have to accept the good with the bad. The positive elements are: she's good looking, very bright, very energetic . . . (Charlene winked at all of us) and once in a while she gives me a break by going to visit her family."

"And the bad news?" I was curious.

"There isn't any, Corey. Absolutely none." Charlene seemed so pleased with herself.

"You're a lecherous peri-menopausal woman, Charlene. Now let's change the subject before we scare Kinshasa out of her shoes." Simone again took charge.

"I'm fine, girls, really. I don't scare easily. I can hold my own. Besides, you might all find yourselves as thinly disguised characters in my next novel."

I held up my glass to toast Kinshasa.

"That will be a trip. To your next novel! And to the fun of doing research!"

"I'm just kidding. I'm not doing research.But, I do have a question. I was wondering if the university had any kind of an organized gay student support group."

Simone shot me a look as she got up to walk toward the kitchen. She was as surprised as I was by Kinshasa's concern.

"Yes, there is a Gay-Straight Student Alliance. It's a couple of years old now. The faculty rep is in the School of Social Work. Right Corey?"

"Yeah. A guy named Frank Windom. I've met with him a couple of times about some lesbian specific issues. Why do you ask?" I hoped my question wasn't too probing.

"Well, I've recently heard some anti-gay remarks on the campus."

I felt my interest meter come to life with this turn in the conversation.

"Were the remarks directed at *you* about your novel?"

"No. Not at all. They were about gay students in general."

"From other students?"

I can't say that I was surprised to hear Kinshasa mention this. But I was disappointed. Now the four of us were pulled into the discussion. Charlene's interest in the football game was dead and buried.

"This was a remark that another teacher made to me about gay people."

Simone interrupted. "Let me guess. Dr. Potato-head, the chairman of our department?"

"Simone, Dr. George doesn't believe that gays and lesbians really exist. He thinks we're all literary devices." I'd come to the conclusion that the man was not stupid, just a victim of his own sheltered parochial life.

"No. It wasn't Dr. George."

"Then it could only be that ass-wipe, Carter Washington." Charlene spoke with certainty.

Kinshasa seemed to be making a decision of some sort.

"I'd rather not identify the person. But I was curious about where a student could complain if there were a question of anti-gay bias, that's all."

"I would think that filing an official complaint with the Dean of Students would be the first step." Karin looked at us for confirmation.

"Probably." Charlene nodded in agreement. "I'm sure that I can speak for all of us when I say that we would rush to file a complaint and to seek a remedy if any of us were victimized by gender or sexual bias."

This time, I raised my glass of wine to toast us all.

"Ladies, I hate to interrupt such a serious subject but if you're all hungry, dinner is ready." Simone summoned us and looked Kinshasa's way.

"This is your first special meal here. So let me explain the ground rules to you. Karin and I put everything out on the kitchen table, including the wine and the other beverages. Then everybody picks up a plate and helps themselves to as much as they want as many times as they want. Okay?"

"That sounds great."

This was turning out to be a better Thanksgiving day than I had imagined it would be. My friends' home was warm and welcoming, the conversation was interesting, the wine was especially good and everyone, including Kinshasa, was relaxed. She didn't seem so uptight around me as she once had. And she seemed fine with Charlene, also. Maybe the times we've spent together working on the Jefferson High project were responsible for her more laid back demeanor. Whatever the reason, I was glad for it. I could see that she could be fun to be with when she was less rigid and uncomfortable.

"So listen guys, the three of you are working so hard on the high school writing project." Simone's gaze took in Charlene, Kinshasa and me. "How's it going?"

I stopped chewing and looked off into space reflectively.

"I think pretty well. But sometimes I wonder if I'm really comunicating with the students."

"That's normal, Corey." Kinshasa supported me. "Don't give up. They'll surprise you."

"I hope so."

"Does it feel like the Jefferson faculty is behind your efforts, Charlene?"

"Definitely. The teachers we're working with are terrific, even Oliver Sullivan, right Kinshasa?"

Kinshasa laughed as she thought about her Jefferson counterpart.

"Yes, even Oliver is coming around."

"You know, Simone, you *could* have had the high school administrator's viewpoint right here at your table today."

Charlene punctuated her remark with her upheld fork. "But . . . *you* chose not to."

Confused and showing it, Kinshasa and I looked at Charlene for some explanation.

"I told Simone that she and Karin should reach out with their sisterly generosity and extend the dinner invitation to Marsha Riley, who told me that she didn't have any plans for today."

Simone assumed her sassy stance.

"And I told Charlene that it's bad manners to tell the hosts whom they should invite. Besides, we don't even *know* Marsha Riley. And this is the north, not the south. We're not in the habit of inviting strangers to our home."

Charlene protested.

"But you know Marsha by reputation. And don't *tell* me that Corey hasn't mentioned her to you."

"Keep me out of this please, Charlene."

I got up to get more mashed potatoes. So I'll swim an extra lap in the university pool to get rid of the extra carbs. Right now I was more intent on Kinshasa's not seeing my embarrassment than thinking I was overeating.

Karin returned to the table just in time to stumble into the conversation.

"Yeah, she *has* mentioned a Marsha somebody to us. Is that the hot principal you said you could be interested in, Corey? The one who flirts with you?"

I yelled from the dining room.

"No. She's not a principal. She's an *assistant* principal." I hoped my short answer would discourage Karin from any further questions.

"Whatever. We've never met her. So we felt funny inviting her to come to Thanksgiving dinner." It was clear that Simone was trying to put a period on the conversation and end it.

Charlene looked at me, pityingly.

"I was just thinking about our Corey, that's all. I was trying to look out for her."

"Sounds like you've got such loyal friends, Corey." Kinshasa made her contribution to a conversation that was clearly uncomfortable for me. I couldn't tell if she were teasing me or if she were being sincere. I leaned toward the former, since she'd already teased me once about how much I flirt with Marsha. There had to be some way to put this topic to bed.

Desperate to divert the talk away from the assistant principal and our mutual flirtation, I looked directly at Kinshasa.

"Kinshasa, what do you think about Karin's and Simone's culinary talents? They've got skills, don't they?"

"Indeed. Everything was delicious." I felt Kinshasa's calm but appraising gaze linger on me, and I didn't know how to interpret that.

"Wait til you've tasted Corey's sweet potato pie, Kinshasa. Talk about cooking skills." Karin went to the kitchen to get the coffee and dessert.

"Oh stop." I held up my hands in mock protest. "All that praise goes right to my head."

My friends must have enjoyed the pie, though. By the time the second one was sliced and the pieces were wrapped to travel, all I had left to carry were the two empty pie plates. Our dinner party was winding down along with our conversation and our energy.

"You two have outdone yourselves. It was another wonderful Thanksgiving feast." I hugged both Simone and Karin. "Thank you."

"Our pleasure, Corey. Thank you for dessert."

Now it was Charlene's turn to embrace the hosts.

"Do you guys want some help with the dishes?"

"No honey. The dishwasher will do the honors. But thanks for offering, and thanks for the wine."

"You're welcome. And you'll notice that I did not drink for two after all. So I can drive myself home."

Karin touched Kinshasa on her shoulder.

"We hope that you'll come back soon. You're always welcome in our home."

"I'm very grateful that you invited me to spend the day with you. With all of you." Kinshasa beamed at us.

Simone grabbed Kinshasa's arm.

"Whew! That's a relief. Charlene didn't frighten you with any of her talk about her love life?"

"Not in the least. And I got a kick out of her making Corey blush when she brought up Marsha Riley."

I zipped my jacket and tried to give Kinshasa a condescending look. I would have succeeded if my glare hadn't been highjacked by one of the sexiest flirtatious smiles I'd ever received. I swallowed hard and tried to not stammer.

"Well, troops. Time to hit the road."

Charlene, Kinshasa and I walked the length of the path to the street together. Then Kinshasa peeled off to the right toward her car. Charlene and I turned left.

"Let's wait til we see Kinshasa get into her car."

"How gallant of you, Corey."

We waited for half a minute until we saw Kinshasa's car's headlights illuminate the space in front of her.

"Now that it's just the two of us, I have a small bone to pick with you, dear Char. Why did you bring up that mess about wanting Simone to invite Marsha to this dinner?"

"You're lucky I didn't quote Simone verbatim, honeycakes."

"What exactly did she say?"

"That there was no way in hell they were going to invite Marsha when it's Kinshasa you were interested in."

"Oh for God's sake. That's old news. It's a dead issue."

"I don't think that *Simone* is convinced there's nothing happening. And you know what, Corey? I watched you today, maybe more than I've watched you in a long time. *You* might believe that your attraction to Kinshasa is a dead issue. But *I* can tell you that it is not."

TWENTY-SEVEN

I was busy at my desk in the office, so I let the phone ring twelve times, convinced that whoever was calling would hang up. Purposely I hadn't ordered call waiting or any of the university's telephone upgrades. I liked telling people that I had "line's busy . . . call again", or, "not here now . . . try later on".

After the thirteenth ring, my patience broke and I picked up the receiver. Jennifer was on the other end, sounding annoyed and impatient.

"Corey? It's Jen. Are you doing anything for lunch today?"

"Yes. I'm working through it." My plan was to snack on cookies and a cup of tea while I finished reading some essays.

"What time will you be at home later on? I want to come by and pick up my things."

"That's fine with me. I'll be home by four."

"Good. See you later."

I finished a student conference and closed my door at three-thirty. I could see a light on in Kinshasa's office, so I tapped lightly and called her name.

"Kinshasa. It's me . . . Corey. Are you in there?"

Kinshasa had told me to always announce myself. Otherwise, I couldn't count on her to answer my knock. Apparently, she'd had some kind of run in with our tenured prick, Carter Washington, and after that, she never wanted to be in her office alone with him. When she told me that, her stock immediately rose in my eyes. If the woman wasn't a lesbian, at least she had good taste and good sense.

Kinshasa didn't answer my knock. I was a little disappointed because I had an article I wanted to show her about a young African-American filmmaker from Philly. Also, I missed checking out what she was wearing today. She had an amazing wardrobe. I don't know if I'd seen her wear the same outfit twice. That's what royalties from the mainstream publishing world can do for you, I suppose.

I trundled on home, tired but anxious for Jennifer to arrive, gather her things and leave. At about four-thirty my doorbell rang. There was Jennifer, standing on the porch with a bag tucked under her arm.

"Hi!" Jennifer stepped into the foyer and hugged me. I tried to hug her back with my best imitation of a straight woman hug . . . my body a foot away from hers, a lot of shoulder and back patting.

"I've already packed your books, tapes and CD-ROM's in boxes. We just have to put them in your car."

Jennifer took a bottle of wine out of the bag.

"I thought that we could have a drink, and maybe go out for dinner."

That creepy trapped feeling of being manipulated was starting to take hold.

"The dinner idea is definitely out, Jen. I'm too tired." I could see the look of disappointment in her eyes.

"But a glass of wine would be nice. Give me the bottle, and I'll pour two glasses while you start bringing the boxes downstairs."

"You packed all the books that I left in our bedroom?"

"You bet."

I wanted to add, "Why the hell would I have left things in 'our' bedroom, if it isn't 'our' bedroom anymore?" But, I didn't.

By the time I came back with the two glasses, Jennifer had settled into the den and opened one of the boxes. She had taken her shoes off and was kneeling on the floor, sorting tapes.

"I still love this room. It's so warm and cozy."

"How's Pat?"

"She's all right. She's been doing a lot of overtime recently, working with an anti-violence program at the high school."

I thought about the odor of violence that I smelled every time I entered Jefferson High, and Jennifer kept talking.

"She's excellent in a crisis. She knows exactly what to say to calm people down. So they took her out of the Special Victims Unit and reassigned her to this new project."

"Do you worry less now about her safety?" I was sincerely interested. Jennifer had bitten off a lot, falling in love with a cop.

"No, not really. I read all the newspaper articles about kids bringing automatic weapons to school . . . and she's not working in the best neighborhood in Philadelphia. Then . . . there are those night meetings she goes to, to talk to parents and community leaders."

"That must leave you with time on your hands?" I suddenly understood why Jennifer was at my door this evening.

"Yeah. And what about you? Do you have a lot of free time now?"

"Absolutely none. I'm working on Charlene's project at Jefferson High in the city."

"I don't believe it, Corey! Jefferson is Pat's school! That's where she's assigned! Haven't you seen her there?"

"No, but I'm there only once or twice a week. And, it's a huge place." I began putting the tapes back into their box.

"I've heard good things about that project, but I never knew it was at Jefferson." Jen sipped some wine before continuing. "You and Kinshasa Jordan are the two Allerton teachers there, right?"

"Uh-huh. She used to teach in a high school, so I lean on her for advice." I thought that I'd better not mention that Jefferson had a gay assistant principal.

Jennifer looked around the room, and then back at me. "Are you sure you don't have time for dinner?"

"I'm positive." I took the last sip of my wine.

"So what's Jordan like when you get to know her?"

Not missing a beat, I answered, "Competent, talented and . . . and straight as the proverbial arrow."

"That's not what *I* heard. The straight part, that is."

"Nor I, but I guess we heard wrong. I was in her apartment once and I overheard her talking to her ex-boyfriend. His name is Michael."

I bent down to secure the filled box.

"So maybe RESIST NOW! knew what they were doing when they protested at her reading."

"I'm not so sure about that. She's straight, but I don't think that she's narrow."

Jennifer was as determined to continue this interrogation as I was to finish it.

"Have you really gotten to know her?"

"Not very well."

I wanted to change the topic. Of all the people I tried to fool about my on again-off again attraction to Kinshasa, Jennifer was the most difficult. I was afraid that she could still see right through me.

"We work together, that's all. I see her on campus and at Jefferson, but we don't socialize much with each other."

"I remember when we 'just worked together'." Jennifer would not be mollified.

"That was different, Jen. *We're* both lesbians." I succeeded in stamping my voice with the tone of finality.

Jennifer stood up and slipped her shoes back on. "Okay. I'll take everything out to my car."

"I'll help, and we can do this in two or three trips."

We loaded the boxes into the trunk and slammed it shut. Jennifer placed her hand atop mine as I gave her the car key.

"How about a quiet dinner, Corey? We could go to that Italian restaurant at the edge of town."

"Sorry, Jen, but I can't."

"Then why don't we go back inside and finish the wine?" Jennifer moved closer to me, her intentions clear.

I felt suffocated by her willingness to spend time and intimacy with me. Time and intimacy that, by all rights, belonged to Pat now.

"Jennifer, I do believe that *I* have more respect for your relationship with Pat than *you* do."

She looked annoyed with me and then got into her car, driving off without another word. I returned to the den and picked up the two used wine glasses. As I headed toward the kitchen, I felt released, free. Free of Jennifer's belongings, and free of her manipulations.

TWENTY-EIGHT

"**S**hit! I'm gonna be late again." Pat jerked the stick shift into second gear and pointed the Jeep toward the city. She didn't want her lateness to encourage any suspicion that much of the time, she was living at Jennifer's apartment, outside the city limits. The commute from Jen's was only thirty-five minutes, if Pat left on time. But a five or a ten minute delay thickened the traffic and made a late arrival a sure thing.

Nevertheless, Pat didn't want to change her wake up time. What did change was the ease with which she could leave Jennifer. As their relationship ripened, Jen began to trust Pat less and less, although Pat had given Jen no reason to doubt her fidelity. More often than not, breakfast had become coffee and an argument. Jennifer suspected Pat of seducing every other woman she came in contact with during the course of doing her job. Pat suspected Jennifer of feeling unnecessarily guilty about leaving Corey, and, at times, of missing that relationship.

Today was another one of those heated mornings. They'd skipped coffee altogether. A good twenty minutes behind schedule, Pat decided to go directly to Jefferson High instead of stopping for something to eat. She'd already spent three entire days at the high school this week, trying to resolve a gang dispute that threatened to explode into something much bigger.

Then there was Tashna Barnett. Pat wanted one more crack at convincing the seventeen year old to press charges against her abusive boyfriend. When Pat first interviewed her, Tashna had nodded a mute "yes", she would file a complaint. Through tears and a swollen split lip, Tashna described how Kareem had punched her the night before. How it wasn't the first time that he had visited violence upon her.

The first time was when she was pregnant with his baby, and wanted to get an abortion. Kareem had broken her nose then. The second time, he got mad for no reason at all, and kicked her in the belly. Said he would give her "the goddam abortion" himself. This last time was the third assault. This time, she was scared. He hadn't even seemed to be angry with her. He just pulled back his fist and wailed into the side of her head, then square into her eye and straight through to her mouth til he broke some teeth.

Pat had taken her out of Marsha Riley's office and helped her into the squad car. By the time the paperwork was finished, Tashna's empty eyes and defeated torso wanted to escape from the refuge of the police station. She refused to sign anything. Too scared. Scared of Kareem. Scared of Kareem's "boys". Scared of his family. Pat knew better than to try to force her into signing the paper work for the arrest warrant. Tashna's fear was all consuming, and she knew that Detective Adamson wouldn't be there for her when Kareem made bail.

Pat pulled into a parking spot in the lot. She walked quickly into the building and to the assistant principal's office, where she paced in front of the closed door. Finally, it opened, belching out an obscenity screaming parent. A young girl, probably the mad woman's daughter, looked straight through Pat as she absorbed the litany of her mother's tirade. Pat watched them grow smaller and smaller in their retreat toward the exit. She stepped across Marsha's threshold.

"Good morning. Looks like your day is off to a rollicking start."

Marsha returned the greeting. "Looks like today is going to be a buster. How can I help you, Detective?"

"I thought I'd make one final attempt to talk Tashna Barnett into charging her boyfriend with assault."

"You're persistent. I'll say that about you. Let me call her out of class. Why don't you sit down until she gets here?"

"Thanks." Pat stood to the side while Marsha found Tashna's roster in her data base and then phoned a classroom. She liked the assistant principal's efficiency, and she figured that her job was as stressful as a cop's.

There was constant foot traffic through Marsha's door. Two people needed her signature on forms. A couple of students and their parents awaited post-suspension interviews. Public address announcements mingled with ringing telephones. Marsha handled all of the confusion with ease, smiling graciously, always listening to more than one thing at a time.

She was assuring Pat that Tashna was on her way, when the first security request buzzed past their ears. Pat looked beyond the office door and saw Tashna in the distance, dawdling toward them, as the second security request staccatoed through the air. Marsha split her attention between the code, Tashna's approach and her suddenly animated walkie-talkie.

Tashna sat down in front of Pat at the same time that someone frantically tapped out a third emergency code. Marsha shot Pat an unexpected look of desperation.

"Feel free to use my office, Detective." She pointed to her two way radio. "We have three fights going on in different parts of the building. I have to go." Marsha picked up her keys and her radio. Less than a second later, Pat told Tashna to wait there, that she'd be right back. Leaping to her feet, she trailed the static of Marsha's walkie-talkie.

The two women broke into a trot and took a flight of stairs two steps at a time. Not knowing the school's layout all that well, Pat followed her intincts and decided to stick close to Marsha. They ran through a narrow hallway lined with classroom doors that were locked from the inside. Students who had been hanging out in the hall and in the stairwell formed a human wake behind Pat and Marsha.

Pat became aware of a mass of teenagers forming a thick circle around an unknown nucleus. The circle was always moving, to the left or to the right, growing alternately looser, then tighter. An adult, perhaps a school district security guard, yelled something at Marsha. Pat couldn't hear what he said, but she saw the anguish on Marsha's face. Instinctively, she felt for her service revolver, ripping open the leather strap that kept it in place under her jacket, near her left breast. She fingered the safety but didn't release it.

The crowd of screaming, frenzied students swarmed onward, sweeping up Marsha and Pat. Marsha yelled something unintelligible into her radio, seconds before it was stripped from her hand.

Pat focused on the radio thief and reached out to collar her when she felt her body being slammed against a wall. Her head, shoulders and spine absorbed such an impact that she never sensed the hand that reached in and removed her gun in one slick movement. Dazed, she thought she saw the flash of the cold blue-black metal as it reared back. She heard a scream rising through the air, and felt the fire sear through her chest.

The swarm of people disappeared as quickly as it had formed, as if a sudden winter freeze had paralyzed the hive. Sulfur, blood, fear and disbelief billowed throughout the hallway, gushed down the stairs and emptied into the dangerous streets surrounding Jefferson High.

TWENTY-NINE

Jennifer had just finished proofreading the last part of the revised admissions policy when her telephone rang. Johnetta Jones, Pat's partner, was on the other end, barely able to speak. Jennifer listened to Johnetta's quavering voice, shook her head slowly from side to side, hung up the phone and remained stock still, staring into a black hole that threatened to swallow her.

An hour passed. She let the phone ring unanswered, and refused to acknowledge the knocks at her door. Instead, she thought about their first meeting in this very office; about the rush she had felt when she first shook Pat's hand. That first contact had been more like an embrace than the formality of a detective probing a stranger for information about a crime. Jennifer remembered her determination to be coupled with Pat; to be consumed by her. She could still recall the flush of heat that covered her body when they first made love that afternoon in Pat's apartment. Her need to be possessed by Pat had made the act of infidelity so easy for Jennifer. Easy, but not guiltless, not even for someone as self centered as Jennifer was.

Then Jennifer thought about their parting words, spoken less than six hours ago. The heat they had generated this morning was fueled by friction, not passion; by suspicion, not unconditional trust. Why hadn't she accepted Pat's declarations of love?

Jennifer picked up the phone and dialed Corey's number, forgetting that she would be in a class at this hour. She tried to call Charlene, who wasn't in her office either. Now desperate to talk to someone who would understand the depth of her loss, Jennifer felt totally alone in her mourning.

Another hour passed. She turned off her desk lamp, put her coat over her shoulders and walked out to the cold parking lot. A familiar voice called to her.

"Jen! I've been waiting here for you. I knocked on your office door, but you didn't answer. Then I tried calling you, but you didn't pick up your phone. I was so concerned for you that I canceled my class, and decided to wait here near your car." Corey paused and looked carefully at a non-responsive Jennifer. "I heard what happened . . . to Pat. It's all over the radio and TV."

Jennifer stared, empty-eyed, at Corey.

"We argued this morning before she left for work. If she had left home on time, she might have gotten there earlier. She might have been doing something else in some other part of the school. She might still be alive."

"Jen, you can't blame yourself for this. It's not your fault, and you couldn't have stopped it from happening." Corey touched Jennifer's arm. "Why don't you leave your car here? I'll drive you home."

"No. I can drive myself. I need to be at home . . . with Pat's things. I need to feel them . . . to touch them."

"I don't think you should be alone now. I can come over to keep you company. I can call Simone and Charlene. They'll want to be with you, too."

"Maybe tomorrow, but not tonight. I thought I wanted to talk to someone, but I really don't. I just want to sit and think."

She unlocked her car and got in, throwing her briefcase into the empty passenger seat. Before closing the door, she looked up at Corey.

"This is the first time that someone's left me behind. I usually do the leaving."

Corey saw no need to respond. She watched Jennifer pull away and head toward the gate. Jennifer inserted her parking permit card into the automatic lock. The gate swung up and opened. Before the barrier could close again, Jennifer accelerated her way toward the first of many painful, tear filled nights.

THIRTY

Kinshasa labored over the final page of her letter to Gayle. The first part flowed effortlessly. She wrote about her students at Allerton, her run in with Carter Washington, the writing project at Jefferson High and the horror of Pat Adamson's death at the school, the Thanksgiving dinner with her new friends. Now, she dragged her pen through the embarrassment of the RESIST NOW! demonstration at the bookstore. She reported the event itself matter of factly. What was difficult was the retelling of her rescue by Corey, Karin and Simone and being alone with Corey when Michael had called. Having to describe the accusations of homophobia was a breeze compared to trying to disguise her ever growing feeling that Corey Lomax was beginning to mean something to her.

She stared at the empty expanse on the piece of stationary, knowing that she couldn't end her letter with a simple and stark, "Corey and her two friends saw that I arrived home safely". Gayle knew all her too well. She knew that such an event in her life would have been laden with all kinds of emotions. Ending her epistle like that would only precipitate Gayle's phoning and grilling her. She'd be forced to admit to Gayle and to herself that she was feeling more than a familiarity, but a growing attraction to Corey. It would be better to disclose more in her letter. Better to accept that after seven months away from her old home, and more than a year removed from Michael's alternating affection and anger, she was being drawn toward a new homecoming in a new place. When Kinshasa stopped denying it, and was able to admit her feelings, she knew that *home* was beginning to look like Corey.

But she had no idea how to begin that journey home to Corey. No notion of how welcoming Corey might be if only she could be honest about how shew felt. Purposely, to protect herself from possible hurt, she'd sent Corey the wrong signals time and time again.

Lately though, Kinshasa found herself looking for Corey at the university, and hoping for a chance to talk with her at the high school. She watched Corey smile at her Jefferson students, and she found herself smiling too. She looked through Corey's open office door, to see her grimacing while she hunched over a stack of ungraded papers, and she longed to reach out and touch her, assuring her that her task wouldn't be all that bad.

But Kinshasa's fear of losing herself in someone else loomed as real as a slap in the face, and it kept her thoughts and longings about Corey just that, thoughts and longings. She'd been abused once by a lover, and she was afraid that she'd go looking for that abuse again. The distance and the ambiguity she'd shown Corey were necessary for her protection. *How in the world* could she find her way home to Corey?

Gradually, Kinshasa filled the letter. She detailed her rescue from Ex Libris, the awkwardness of juggling Michael's call with the intensity of Corey's presence in her kitchen, and the silent drive to Corey's house. She counted on Gayle to fill in any missing pieces and to know how she felt about all of this.

The clock on the mantle wore a microphone as it rhythmically reminded her how late it had become. She was hosting today's "Allerton-Jefferson Six", as they had begun to call themselves, and she had only one hour left to do some final preparations.

Kinshasa went into the kitchen, cut some fruit and arranged it on a platter with cheeses. She sliced French bread and gathered the mulling spices for the apple cider. She had peach cider, also, because she'd heard Corey rave about a juice stand at a local farmers' market.

Methodically, she took out napkins, mugs, small plates and the coffee maker. Marsha Riley had a voracious thirst for coffee. Kinshasa had noticed that every time the group met. Her earlier public amusement with Marsha's thirst for *Corey*, had changed privately into a feeling of annoyance. When she let herself be perfectly honest, she knew that her feelings were pretty damn close to jealousy. She wondered if Corey were still as interested in Marsha as she had been some time ago, when she teased her about her obvious flirting. Fearing what Corey's answer might be kept her from asking. She didn't want to know if they were seeing each other other than at the school or at these group meetings.

With a little more than an hour left before the start of the meeting, Kinshasa stepped into the shower. She shampooed and let the water flow over her head. Leaning back against the cool tile wall, she caressed her body with smooth, soapy hands. Too relaxed to suppress the notion, she thought, simply, "Corey". And Corey's smiling image competed with the waterfall cascading down Kinshasa's length. After a moment, she stood completely erect, pulling herself away from the wall and the want for the woman who occupied her thoughts more and more. Kinshasa chastised herself with every rough stroke of her bath towel. She tried to dry Corey out of her mind.

THIRTY-ONE

Sarah and I arrived at Kinshasa's apartment at the same time. I had to admit that we worked well together. I liked Sarah's "let's do it" attitude, and Sarah felt good about my willingness to learn how to work with younger students. She was a great mentor in a mothering kind of way.

Kinshasa smiled her greeting.

"Come on in and hang your jackets in the closet."

I felt Kinshasa looking at me, and I hoped that my slacks and sweatshirt were presentable. No one ever got dressed up for these meetings, but I didn't want to look disreputable in front of her . . . or Marsha, for that matter.

Sarah walked around the livingroom.

"Kinshasa, your apartment is wonderful! All of these windows must give you great light on a sunny day."

"Thank you Sarah. They do. It's too bad that it's so cloudy today."

I looked out of the largest of the windows and thought that I could spot a light rain beginning to fall. Kinshasa counted the chairs in the livingroom.

"Corey, could you do me a favor? I need two more chairs in here. Could you help me get them? One is in the den, and there's a hassock I'll get from the bedroom."

"Sure. No problem." I followed her to the den and picked up the light weight chair she pointed to.

"So is this where you'll write your next novel?"

"I've barely had a chance to think about the next one, although my agent is pressuring me." She paused, and then added, "How about you? Have you written any short fiction lately?"

I pointed to my head. "There's one up here, but I haven't committed anything to paper yet. Lately, life has been stranger than fiction."

"I know what you mean."

I carried the chair to the doorway. "Can I help you with the hassock?"

"I don't think so." Kinshasa gave me one of her broad smiles. "At least, not with that chair in your arms."

I knew that it was silly of me to follow Kinshasa to the bedroom, instead of simply returning to the living room with the chair, but follow her, I did. I wanted to see her in an intimate place. So I ignored the fact that she hadn't invited me to go with her there. Looking at the quilted floral fabric that covered her bed, I tried to memorize the colors, so that I could add them to my fantasies of Kinshasa the very next time that I forgot that we were only friends, only colleagues. I looked all around the room, trying to take in everything. On her night table was an all too familiar book, mine. I said nothing and did my best not to stare at her. But it was hard to keep my eyes from lingering on hers. Unfortunately, for the part of me that likes to think that I'm smooth and cool, looking at her in this place *and* coming up with something intelligent to say proved to be impossible.

Kinshasa broke the silence. "We'd better take these chairs into the living room."

We were putting the seats in place just as Oliver and Charlene arrived. They walked in with wet umbrellas that Oliver wanted to leave out in the hallway by the apartment door.

"No, that's all right. Put them here in the entryway. A little water won't hurt anything." Kinshasa took the umbrellas from him and put them on the tile floor near the door.

"I'm afraid that we brought the rain with us." Oliver blurted this out as if he were at confession.

"What a surprise." Sarah, whose dry sense of humor was a source of delight to everyone except Oliver, couldn't resist a remark. I saw her look at him and stifle a frown. She had told me more than once that she thought she'd never known anyone so young with such a negative mindset.

Charlene began the meeting without waiting for Marsha to arrive.

"We can discuss some things without Marsha, since it looks like she's going to be late."

"Maybe she had car trouble . . . or she's been in an accident." Oliver offered.

I stole a look at Sarah, who winced, and at Kinshasa. Her expression was inscrutable.

"I seriously hope not, Oliver." Charlene shot me a look and didn't miss a beat.

"Now, I've arranged for the university to print and bind all of the students' work. Their price is well within our budget, and the Fraternal Order of Police is tossing in a nice donation, because the journal will be dedicated to Pat Adamson's memory."

Sarah nodded and added, "And Marsha has cleared the way for the kids to use the word processors in the computer lab during class time, instead of after school. You know how they hate to stay one minute after the last bell."

We heard the phone ring and Kinshasa got up to answer the intercom signal. A moment later Marsha stormed into the foyer, carrying her raincoat cavalierly over one arm. Obviously, this woman enjoys making an entrance.

We all thought that we knew what was on the meeting's agenda, but it was clear that *Marsha* had an agenda of her own. She looked directly at me when she said hello . . . how was everybody, so I figured that *I* was part of her plan.

"Sorry I'm late, but you know what happens as soon as the streets get wet. Traffic was crawling. Now what did I miss so far?"

I was enjoying Marsha's charm. Sarah was tolerant but watchful. Oliver was oblivious to it. And Kinshasa was an easy read. She seemed pissed with Marsha's diva entrance.

"You haven't missed that much." Charlene picked up the pieces of the interrupted flow and repeated what had been said.

The meeting clipped along faster than the traffic on the street four floors below us. We quickly reached a consensus about a lot of the students' writings, and decided to take a break for refreshments.

"You've gone to so much trouble for us, Kinshasa." Sarah got up to help. "The least I can do is help bring the food."

Kinshasa watched me choose one of the two carafes she'd put on the table, and pour a mug of the peach drink.

I smiled triumphantly at her.

"You found it! Did you drive out to Reed's Farmers' Market?"

"Yes, I did. I followed your directions. And I got the fruit and cheeses there, too."

"You should have called me. I would have driven out there with you." I saw Kinshasa's face turn red.

"Peach cider? I've never heard of that. May I taste some of yours, Corey?" Marsha inserted herself between Kinshasa and me, deftly cupped her hands over mine and drew the mug to her mouth.

"This is wonderful! *You* certainly know what tastes good."

Now it was my turn to blush and feel my cheeks burning. Kinshasa turned her attention away from Marsha and me and toward the others. I got up and headed out to the kitchen to refill the carafe. I could sense Marsha following me. All of a sudden I realized how strange the situation was. I'd looked forward to a scene like this happening, ever since I'd met Marsha. But for some reason, I was paying more attention to Kinshasa's whereabouts than to my conversation with the assistant principal. I'm not even sure what we said to each other. I was too busy trying to figure out what Kinshasa was saying to Charlene and to Sarah. But at the end of our little tête-à-tête, Marsha said to me, "Then it's settled. MKDN'S Place at nine o'clock tonight."

"I'll be there." I looked over at Charlene and winked. She was the only other person in the room who knew what MKDN'S Place was. Charlene returned my wink, and then stole a look at Kinshasa.

Our little group reassembled in the living room, refreshed and ready to finish the meeting's business.

"You don't need any more input from me, do you Charlene?" Marsha prepared to leave. She stood up and walked to the coat closet. I was willing to put money on Marsha's exit being as dramatic as was her late entrance.

"No. I don't think so." She looked at the rest of us. "In fact, we're all just about finished for today. We've made the toughest decisions. Anything else for the good of the cause?"

"Yes." Kinshasa's voice was strong and strident as she turned her gaze directly to me. "I'd like to talk with Corey for a few more minutes. There are a few details about the editing and the portfolios that I need to discuss with you. Can you stay for a moment longer?"

"Sure." I couldn't refuse such a forceful request, although I was anxious to go home and contemplate my date with Marsha.

"And I'll help you take the chairs back to the other rooms if you'd like."

"That's not necessary. I can do that by myself." Kinshasa's tone was not getting any softer.

"Kinshasa, I'll see you at school next Tuesday." Marsha tightened the belt of her raincoat. "MKDN'S a little later, Corey?"

"You bet."

Charlene telegraphed me a "what's up?" look as she walked out the door. I answered her with a shrug. The others put on their jackets and hurried to ride the elevator that Marsha had summoned.

I waited for Kinshasa to close the door.

"What's up? Is anything wrong with the portfolios?" I scanned her face, searching for a clue. She just stared back at me, as if she were waiting for her annoyance to lessen.

"Kinshasa, uh, what's so important about the editing that it can't wait until we're at school?"

Then I lowered my voice to a mock sexy whisper. "You realize, don't you, that I *cannot* be late for this date with Marsha."

"What's so *important* about your date with Marsha?"

Her question threw me. But I was willing to answer her candidly.

"Let me count the ways. First of all, I like the way that she looks. Second, I like the way that she looks at *me*. And third, I haven't had a *significant* date for over a year now."

I smiled mischievously, totally missing the edge of seriousness in Kinshasa's question.

"And I miss the *significance* of your having a date with her." Kinshasa's voice had become lower, more serious than she wanted it to be.

"May I ask you something, Corey?" She didn't wait for me to say yes or no. "I know that you had a relationship with Jennifer Renfrew. Do you always date white women?"

I wasn't prepared for Kinshasa's aggression.

"In fact, I don't. But since we're talking about my dating habits, you might remember that a few months ago, when I tried to go out with a woman of color, *you* declined my invitation."

Kinshasa glared at me, undaunted by my answer.

"You told me that your invitation to dinner wasn't a date."

"Maybe I wasn't being totally honest with you, or with myself for that matter. The point is, *you* wanted no part of going out with me."

"So *I'm* responsible for your choice of women, simply because I didn't want to go out with you for a drink and dinner? I don't think so." Her face was tinged with anger.

"Quite frankly, *you're* not responsible for any thing in my life, Kinshasa. And I resent your implying that I'm not attracted to Black women. Whose business is it whom I go out with?"

I could see Kinshasa pulling back from her anger.

"You're right, Corey. It's not my business. We don't need to have this conversation at all. You should leave now while you're still on time to meet Marsha at that women's bar.

She went to the closet and got my jacket, handing it to me abruptly.

"Thanks."

I was ready to go, but I didn't want to leave Kinshasa like this. I felt completely turned around and undone. I couldn't understand her anger with me, and I wanted a truce.

"Look, Kinshasa, I don't know how we got to this place, but I'd like to leave feeling at peace with you. We're friends. I don't want to argue with you."

Her face softened.

"Corey, I'm sorry. Really. I'm way out of line, and I apologize. I intruded into your personal business and I shouldn't have." She offered me her hand.

I accepted her apology and her hand and sighed deeply for what might have been. I knew that I didn't want to let go of her. I didn't want to break the little physical contact that we had.

"Good-night, Kinshasa. I guess I'll see you at school."

Sleepwalking down the hallway, I arrived at the elevator and leaned into the button. The door opened, swallowing me and my feelings. I was angry with Kinshasa. More than that, I was confused. I hated the mixed messages she'd sent me these last few months. I hated wanting her to care about me, and being afraid to care about her.

I went out into the wet darkness, crossed the street to my car and slumped into the driver's seat. Sheets of cold, penetrating rain rolled down the windshield as I sat there, mulling over the reality of my unanswered desire to be with Kinshasa, and the hurt of her continual rejection. A friendship with her had not been enough for me, although at one time I'd been willing to settle for that. The sooner the Jefferson High project was completed, the better. I'd only need to run into Kinshasa in the department office or in the classroom building where we both taught.

I put the key into the ignition, mentally replaying our argument. Damn it! Why does she care that I'm meeting Marsha Riley at MKDN'S? And how does she know that it's a women's bar?

Looking up at the fourth floor of her apartment building, I knew that I'd never have another opportunity like the one in front of me; another chance to go after someone I truly wanted. I had to risk her anger and rejection. Now.

So, I left my car and re-crossed the street. Once inside the vestibule, I picked up the security phone and dialed Kinshasa's memorized number. I felt disconnected from my voice, and mumbled, "It's me, Kinshasa. Please let me in."

The door buzzed its permission to enter. I rested against the rear wall of the elevator as it lifted me slowly to her floor. When I arrived at her apartment, Kinshasa was there, holding the door open. Sade's "No Ordinary Love" poured from the cd player on the bookshelf next to the fireplace.

She held me in her gaze. "Did you forget something?"

All of her earlier fight had deserted her.

I stepped into the foyer, passing by Kinshasa very closely, and smelling that same fragrance she'd left, like an echo, in my home the night of the reception.

"Yes. I've forgotten a lot of things lately. Like being persistent when I want something or *someone* very badly."

Kinshasa looked down at the floor, then back up at me, cautious but without censure. I searched her face and stopped at her eyes. Without asking if I could, I leaned toward Kinshasa and kissed her gingerly on her mouth. Her lips formed a silent "no", so I stepped back in deference to her refusal.

"Please, Kinshasa. I want you. Spending time so close to you, but not being able to *be* with you is taking the very breath out of me."

"Being with me would be a mistake." Her eyes held such sadness.

"I keep searching for the mistake, but you seem so right."

Now it was Kinshasa who took a step backward. Her eyes flashed defensively.

"How can you want to be with me *and* with Marsha Riley at the same time?"

"I don't really want to be with Marsha. But you haven't given me half a chance to really know you." I was closer to pleading with Kinshasa than I'd ever been with any woman. And I didn't give a damn. I didn't care about how I sounded, how desperate I seemed.

Kinshasa shook her head vehemently. Her eyes flashed with sudden anger.

"I don't believe you, Corey. Thirty minutes ago, you were hot to meet Marsha at that bar. You didn't want to be late for your *significant* date. Remember? You know your *date* would have ended in your bed or hers."

"Kinshasa Jordan, I don't believe you just said that." I spoke quietly, evenly. And I smiled faintly at the picture her anger had painted.

She didn't answer right away. She walked over to the window and stared out at the rain. Seconds later, she wheeled around.

"I said it, and I mean it, Corey! You'd fuck Marsha in a New York minute. And then, you'd try your best to get me into bed. Inevitably, you'd screw over both of us!"

I approached Kinshasa and spoke calmly, as if our lives depended upon my next words.

"I'm not Michael, you know. It sounds like you're describing his behavior."

"You're right. You're not Michael. But Michael taught me some valuable lessons."

Kinshasa had an answer for everything I said to her.

"Michael taught you pain."

"Pain and not to trust anyone with my feelings."

I stepped closer to her. "You could try trusting a woman."

"I've tried that already. Michael *is* a woman." The fire in Kinshasa's voice extinguished itself.

I gave her words time to filter through my mind and go to my heart. I chanced touching her cheek with my fingertips, tentatively, softly, yet determined to continue.

"I'm going to kiss you again, Kinshasa, because I can't be this close to you and not kiss you. Wanting to be with you without being able to hurts too much."

Very lightly and delicately, I covered Kinshasa's mouth with my own. This time, her lips telegraphed their assent. This time, when I looked into her eyes, I saw a world of hurt, but the promise of a new life; the suspicion and fear that I was the bearer of future pain, but the hope that I was not.

Kinshasa placed both of her hands on my face, outlining my cheekbones, and coming to rest on my mouth. I kissed each finger, made a shelter of my arms and circled Kinshasa, pulling her close to me. Barely speaking, my voice muffled by months of wanting her, I breathed out the words, "I want you. Please trust me."

Raindrops clinging to the living room windows photographed Kinshasa draping her arms over my shoulders, and opening her mouth to meet my kisses. She pulled away, only to find my hand and lead me through the hallway.

I followed Kinshasa until we reached the darkened bedroom. My legs threatened to buckle under the weight of the realization that what I had wanted to happen for so long was about to begin. So many times I had imagined undressing Kinshasa, slowly, enjoying the disappearance of each piece of clothing. But it was Kinshasa who took charge, pulling my jacket off, and then my sweatshirt up and over my head. She smiled her appreciation when she saw that I was not wearing a bra. She kissed both breasts, awakening my nipples.

I unbuttoned Kinshasa's shirt and slipped it off, past her shoulders and arms. Very gently, I removed her bra. Kinshasa's breasts were as I had imagined: rounded, the color of burnished copper, accented by darker nipples that were growing with her desire for our lovemaking.

I looked at Kinshasa and saw her eyes lose their defensiveness and melt into wanting. We began kissing, tentatively at first, and then, almost uncontrollably. Kinshasa's throat vibrated with barely audible sounds. So great was my want that I was headed over the edge.

"Please make love to me, Corey."

I unzipped Kinshasa's slacks and guided them and her panties to the floor. She hooked her thumbs in the belt loops of my jeans and eased them down and over my hips. Together we removed them completely and smiled at each other shyly but knowingly when we felt how wet my panties had become.

We began to kiss again, determined to touch every inch of each other. I held Kinshasa's hips, caressing them as I bent down and made small bites on her rounded stomach. With my tongue, I drew small circles around her navel. I listened, passion building as Kinshasa called out my name.

Barely able to stand, we moved to the bed. I guided her onto it, never interrupting my kisses, never ceasing the caresses. I moved my hand from Kinshasa's hips to her thighs. She understood my message, and opened herself to welcome my loving.

"Corey, I want you so much. I want you inside of me."

I lost my mind with that invitation. My eyes misted over with the wonder that we were creating. As the moisture of our lovemaking moved down my leg, I entered Kinshasa's center with one finger, and then with two. I moved in and out of her with passion's grace, stroking her in her most tender place. Wracked with feeling, Kinshasa wrapped her legs around my waist. Our pleasure was building to such a fine intensity.

"I'm loving you so much, Kinshasa. Baby, I can't stop myself from coming."

"Corey!" Kinshasa lost all of any control she'd ever truly had.

We lay together, facing each other. Our bodies were merged by sweat and sweet sexual secretions. When Kinshasa looked at *me*, I willed her to see the calm sea, even as she continued to shudder from the storm of our lovemaking. When I looked at *her*, I saw clear to the bottom of the ocean. In Kinshasa's eyes, I saw all the refuge that love promised, all the joy and freedom that we had earned by taking this one last chance to find each other.

We pulled the bed covers near, and I asked Kinshasa if I could stay for the night. She smiled her assent and we slept peacefully, nearly until dawn, when we awoke and rolled into lovemaking once again. It was good. It was so very good for both of us.

THIRTY-TWO

I could sense that Kinshasa was in her office, even before I smelled her perfume or heard her voice talking on her phone. It was as if every sense that I had was attuned to her. I had fallen completely in love with Kinshasa Jordan. The months of denial and protestations to my friend Simone had only increased my urge to love this woman. We spent as much time together as possible, talking, listening to each other, learning everything we could about each other. And of course, we spent so much time loving each other. We never simply had sex. We always made love. Sometimes we were in a furious rush . . . grabbing, pulsing, screaming one another's names. At other times we touched each other slowly, caressing lightly, whispering, tasting, enjoying the pleasure of how our touches felt to each other. No matter how we made love, though, every time was an opportunity to grow the mutual trust that was growing between us.

I liked to remember the first time that I saw Kinshasa, at the Luna Negra on a Sunday early last March. It was the same day that I spotted the spring bulbs that had burst into bloom in my back yard. Now, it's mid December. And while I usually dread the approach of winter, all I can think about is how warm we'll be as we grow closer together.

As soon as I saw the light on in Kinshasa's office, I knocked on her door.

"It's me, Kinshasa." I nudged the door open just as Kinshasa swung around in her chair.

"Hey . . . come on in. Good morning."

"Hello, baby." I whispered my greeting, aware of the thin walls and the even thinner veneer of tolerance at the university. "I missed you last night."

"I missed you, too, honey. But staying at my place was the only way I was going to have time to work on my grades. There are too many distractions when I'm alone with you." Kinshasa sent me a teasing look. "Do you have time to sit down and have a cup of coffee with me?"

"I'm afraid not. Besides, we're safer with me standing a few feet away from you. If I get any closer, I can't be responsible for my actions."

I looked at her tenderly, wanting to hold her. I was one second away from stepping closer and exploring her mouth with mine. This was one of those times when I didn't care who might see or hear us. I took a deep breath.

"Did you finish your grades?"

"Yes. I emailed them to the records office about an hour ago."

"Good. So we're on for tonight?"

"Tonight? Are we supposed to see each other tonight?"

Kinshasa winked at me.

"Well, I could check my schedule. But I believe that I penciled you in for dinner. Today is Friday, right?"

I flashed her a smile. She couldn't out-tease me.

"It is. What time should I be there?"

"I'll be there by three. How about three-o-one?"

"Dr. Lomax, isn't that a little early for dinner?"

I walked over to her, bent down and blew into her ear.

"Dinner is at six. You're the appetizer, baby. I want you to be at my front door at three o'clock, and in my arms by three o'one."

Kinshasa smiled and turned her head very slightly toward me. Her mouth was just inches from mine.

"I wouldn't miss it for the world. I'd ask about dessert, but I don't want Dr. George to come in and have to fire us."

"Yeah. Unemployment isn't pretty. So I'll tell you all about dessert when I see you."

I inhaled her fragrance as I stepped away.

"Better pack your boots. We're supposed to get some snow later on."

"You cook and forecast the weather, too? I'm impressed."

"You'd better be impressed, woman." I felt myself slipping into seriousness. "You know, Kinshasa, since we've been seeing each other, I've become so much better than I used to be."

"Is 'seeing each other' what we're doing, Corey?" Kinshasa matched my serious tone with her own.

"It's much more than that, and we both know it."

I stroked the side of her face.

"I'll see you about three o'clock, honey."

"Yes you will."

THIRTY-THREE

Kinshasa sat at her desk in the apartment and sorted her mail, tossing the circulars into the waste basket and stacking the bills and a letter from Gayle to her right. She spotted an envelope from her landlord. It was too early in the month to send in her rent, so she figured that this was a letter about renewing her lease. No one at the university had said anything to her about extending her visiting professor contract, nor about changing her status there. And she needed to contact the New Haven School District about her leave of absence. She had to make some decisions soon. And she needed to talk to Corey, without pressuring her about their relationship. If there were any doubts that Corey had . . . any reservations about their continuing to see each other . . . There was *no* doubt in Kinshasa's mind that she wanted permanence with Corey.

She glanced at her watch and couldn't believe the time. It was already two forty-five. The drive to Corey's would take at least twenty minutes, the way that afternoon traffic dragged along. She smiled as she thought about how Corey refers to Allerton's afternoon traffic flow. She calls it "senior speed trap", because all of the senior citizens are out driving between ten a.m. and four o'clock p.m. Not one of them is exceeding twenty-five miles per hour. If you happen to get stuck behind one of them, you're in "the trap". Kinshasa teased Corey that the two of them would be part of that age group before they knew it.

She'd left her briefcase in the trunk of the car, so all she had to do was grab a change of clothes, and put it in her over-nighter. Always anxious to make enough time to be with Corey, Kinshasa had learned the fine art of reducing a half dozen domestic chores into one continuous motion. She remembered that Corey was fixing salmon for dinner, so she grabbed a bottle of chardonnay. Quickly glancing out the window, she noticed that a light snow had begun falling. She threw on her jacket and scooped up her boots just as the intercom's buzzer sliced the air. Maybe it was a delivery. She was expecting some books from Gerald's store.

Kinshasa put down her boots so that she could push the intercom button.

"Yes?"

There was some static, then she heard the voice.

"Kinshasa? It's me."

Kinshasa froze, her finger poised above the intercom control. She pressed it down.

"What are you doing here, Michael? What do you want?"

"To see you for a few minutes."

Her mind raced. She knew it would be smarter to see Michael in the lobby, instead of alone in her apartment. A public place might discourage her from staging an emotional scene.

"Stay there. I'll be down in a minute."

She picked up her boots and made sure that her keys were in her jacket pocket. Hoisting the over-night bag over her shoulder, she marched to the elevator and descended to the lobby. When she emerged, she could see Michael, peering through the vestibule's door window. Kinshasa strode over and opened the door. Michael tried to embrace her, but Kinshasa stepped back.

"It's so good to see you, baby." Michael looked at Kinshasa and wet her lips in anticipation of kissing her.

Kinshasa stared back, trying to recall what had attracted her to Michael in the first place.

"I can't return the compliment."

Michael cocked her head to one side, ready to work her old fail proof charm. "You look as good as I remember, baby."

Kinshasa stood toe to toe with her.

"I hope that you remember everything, Michael. Because the last time that you saw me, I had blood dripping from my face."

Michael looked down at the tile floor, summoning her much rehearsed expression of contrition.

"I'm so sorry about that, Kinshasa. I've changed, you know what I'm saying? I'm not the same Michael that I used to be."

"I've changed too."

Silence shrouded them.

Michael strightened her head and shifted gears. Her eyes grazed Kinshasa's body from her head down to her feet.

"Looks like you're on your way somewhere. Want company . . . or do you already have some?" A slight leer took its place on her face.

"I *am* going somewhere. And no, I don't want your company." Kinshasa didn't keep the impatience out of her voice.

"So let's end this conversation quickly."

"Quickly? I've driven all the way down here from New Haven. And you want to rush me?" Michael's voice grew louder with her impatience and lack of success.

"That's on you Michael. No one invited you here, you know."

Michael held her hands up defensively.

"Okay. Okay. I'll accept that from you."

She moved closer to Kinshasa, who stood her ground.

"If you'll hear me out, you just might want to change your mind about wherever you're going, honey."

Kinshasa wished this wasn't happening. She pictured Corey in her home waiting for her to arrive. She could feel Corey's arms encircling her waist, and she imagined that melting sensation as Corey's hands slowly caressed her hips, pulling Kinshasa closer to her. That's where she longed to be, where she had a right to be. Not here in this lobby, but in Corey's arms. She leveled her gaze at Michael and lowered her voice to a controllable rage.

"Hear me out, Michael. There is absolutely no one on this earth who could change my mind about where I'm going. If you think that I am the least bit interested in you, after the way that you abused me, then you are out of your damn mind."

She paused long enough to catch her breath.

"This is the last time that I'm going to say this to you. I do not love you. I don't even *like* you. And if you come here again, I'll get a restraining order against you."

Michael's mouth took on a strange grin.

"Yeah, I can see that *you've* changed, Kinshasa. You're not even giving me a chance to talk to you. You're just mouthing off."

Now it was Michael's turn to come up for air.

"You know all those times that I called you a bitch? I didn't know what a bitch was. But you're showing me now, aren't you?"

She glared menacingly at Kinshasa, took a couple of steps backwards, and then came forward again, quickly, so close that Kinshasa could feel the waves of Michael's body heat radiating to her.

"And you think I hit you hard before? You don't *know* what hard is."

Her hands knotted into fists.

Kinshasa let her boots fall to the floor. She stood as erectly as she could.

"Go ahead, Michael! Hit me! Show me how much you've changed, damn it!"

Michael glared at Kinshasa, then dropped her fists and began to plead.

"You can't leave us like this, Kinshasa! Look, I know I was wrong, and that I hurt you. I'm sorry. I apologize. I want you back. Please, baby."

"Go on back to Connecticut, Michael. I have a life *here*, now, and I'm happy."

Aching for Corey's presence, Kinshasa picked up her boots and stepped around Michael. She walked out into the snow and toward her car, never looking back. Instead, she drove away slowly, having no doubt that she was doing the right thing.

THIRTY-FOUR

"Corey? I'm here."

Kinshasa let herself in, closing the front door to Corey's home. She arrived a half an hour after her confrontation with Michael. Shaken and preoccupied with how close she had come to feeling another blow from Michael's fist, she had taken her time and had driven slowly on the snow slicked streets of Allerton.

"I'm in the den, baby." Corey stood up from her desk and met Kinshasa at the doorway to the room. "What took you so long? I've been waiting for you."

They lingered through a kiss, Kinshasa cradling Corey's face with her hands.

"It's a long story . . . I'll tell you about it later."

"Come on out to the kitchen with me. We can make dinner together."

Corey put her arm around Kinshasa's waist, pulling her close and reveling in how warm and welcoming her body felt through her clothing as they walked down the short hallway together.

"I brought a bottle of wine, honey. Here." Kinshasa handed the bottle to Corey. "What are we having with the salmon?"

"How about some rice and a salad?"

"That sounds good."

"Want to be in charge of the salad?"

"I think I can handle that."

As Kinshasa washed the salad greens in the sink, she looked out of the window at the snow falling silently on the ring of stately evergreens bordering the backyard.

"Your yard is beautiful, even in the winter. I remember how lush everything was last June when you had my 'welcome to Allerton' party."

She turned around and faced Corey.

"Simone did such a good job of advertising your gardening talents. She could be your agent, you know."

"Sometimes I think that she is."

"She pointed out all of the flower beds that you've established since you moved here, and all of the trees and shrubs. She even had me visualizing the Spring flowers."

"Yeah. That's Simone. She and Karin have given me most of those bulbs as Christmas and birthday presents. They are special gifts, especially after a rough winter."

Kinshasa turned around, wanting to give all of her attention to Corey.

"When do the first bulbs begin to bloom?"

"Usually in early March. But sometimes in late February, if we've had a mild winter."

"And when do the pine trees sprout their new needles?"

"In early May." Corey moved over to Kinshasa, encircling her with her arms. She placed two soft kisses on Kinshasa's neck.

"That's five months from now. Maybe, by that time . . . you'll be living here with me."

Kinshasa looked steadily into Corey's eyes, measuring the sincerity that she saw there.

"I want so much to live here with you, Corey."

She remembered the stack of mail that she'd left on her desk in the apartment, and she knew exactly how she would respond to the lease renewal letter. Perhaps Allerton University would offer her a contract renewal; perhaps not. Either way, she supposed that she would have to write to the New Haven School District, changing her one year leave of absence to a permanent resignation.